Brogan Werder had *Our Back Porch*, a flash fiction, published in Finger Lakes College literary magazine, The Finger. Krysten Layne is her nom de plume. She lives with her husband, Devon, and cat in Rochester, NY. This is her debut novel.

To Devon, my hubby, who supported this endeavor and all my craziness. And to Sharon Sprague, who always asked, "Is it ready yet?"

Krysten Layne

LORD AINSLEY

To Jill

[handwritten inscription and signature]

AUSTIN MACAULEY PUBLISHERS™

LONDON • CAMBRIDGE • NEW YORK • SHARJAH

Ordering Information
Quantity sales: Special discounts are available on quantity purchases by corporations, associations, and others. For details, contact the publisher at the address below.

Publisher's Cataloging-in-Publication data
Layne, Krysten
Lord Ainsley

ISBN 9781647502348 (Paperback)
ISBN 9781645364023 (Hardback)
ISBN 9781647502355 (ePub e-book)

Library of Congress Control Number: 2021900912

www.austinmacauley.com/us

First Published (2021)
Austin Macauley Publishers LLC
40 Wall Street, 33rd Floor, Suite 3302
New York, NY 10005
USA

mail-usa@austinmacauley.com
+1 (646) 5125767

First and foremost, I would like to thank my husband. I began this book when we had just started dating and now, five years into our lives together and because of his support, it is done. I would also like to thank Sharon for being the one who listened to my awful British accent when I read her the first drafts and always believed the book should be published. Thank you to my beta readers who gave me the best gift a budding author could ever ask for: honest critique. Thank you to Miranda Belle-Isle, my first editor, who worked with me through "three" whole rewrites. Thank you to Austin Macauley, who saw the potential and took my book the rest of the way. And thank you, at last, to the readers, who I hope will enjoy this book.

Prologue

The most terrifying part of a man following a woman is the motive. The night is cold, and the street lights are dampened by fog, the bottom of her dress wet, and his shoes muddy. Her body stiffens with the realization that he's been tracking her for a few blocks. He can sense she's aware now, but it doesn't deter him.

Her heart pounds with each step. She can't outrun him or turn to fight; age has robbed her of the strength and fortitude necessary. She must find someone, somewhere, to seek shelter and safety but alas, there are no friendly faces here. No warmly lit doorways in which she would be welcomed. And he is closing in.

She stops midstride to turn, determined to face her fate head on, hoping her boldness may startle him. His pace is brisk, and he is soon upon her. But then, miraculously, he continues past her, his face covered with the shadow of a hat he tips in her direction.

She breathes a weighty sigh, closing her eyes for just a moment as relief washes over her in waves—he strikes her.

The shock steals the scream from her throat and she falls to the ground, her vision blurring. He looms over her and she sees the face uncovered, impassive as he stares at her.

Her mind tries to comprehend the intentions behind his expression, her lips trembling as it begins to rain.

He stoops to pick her up, dragging her into a nearby alley. He does not allow her to speak or cry aloud. No, the time for her is over. It's *his* time now.

Chapter One
Lord Ainsley

His memoirs began when he was a much younger man. Their pages told of a man in his prime, of wanderlust and adventure. He traveled the world, earning his title and satisfying what seemed an unquenchable thirst of curiosity.

On a particular expedition, the memoirs were halted. He returned sooner than expected to his home among the foggy, rain-wet streets of London. And when his memoirs began again, it was clear: a different man now held the pen.

***

'Lord Ainsley III was born into a small family of large fortune in London, 1848. His mother's only child, she kept him close and always with silver spoon in cheek. His father, Lord Ainsley II, was the opposite in every way but one: assuring his only son's survival.

'In a time of dank days and disease, the young boy was kept tucked away from the great big world of danger. Only his trusted butler and the books on his shelf were his window into the outside world. With a father away on business and a mother frittering away in society, what was a young child to distract himself with besides stories?

'Excitement and intrigue, mystery and marvel, legends and myths: these filled his childhood. And in an estate as great as what the Ainsley family had acquired, there was no lack of opportunities for exploration and wonder. Ceaseless baubles sent from distant lands, secret doors leading to chambers unknown, and an accomplice of a butler to sneak unauthorized snacks during breaks from sieges, conquests, thieveries, and the solving of cases. A childhood of privilege to be certain, yet one of deep loneliness.

'It wasn't long before the young master had to abandon his adventures in the name of propriety. Time to trade dirt and play clothes for stiff collars and stiffer buttons, the pleasure of unhindered exploration for the rigidity of proper schooling. Suffice to say childhood does not last long within such an institution.

'I imagine this is the point in Lord Ainsley's life where he transformed from the bright-eyed, innocent boy to the stoic gentleman who would take over the family name. He was no longer a boy running forth with wild ideas, but still driven nonetheless. A son Lord Ainsley II could be proud of. However, you never can rely on people to end up quite the way you first expect. While still attending prep school, Lord Ainsley III suddenly became the only living heir to the Ainsley fortune. All the young master's father had wanted for his son was for him to live. Alas, he must have forgotten to do so himself.

'Time passes much in the way it should. The world seems to move around like you are its center. Then life proves differently.

'Lord Ainsley spent the remainder of his youth in various boarding schools, then continued his studies at a prestigious college where he hoped to firmly grasp his future. I believe here he was offered to study abroad. Study what, I am not certain, but he earned many a degree and auspicious title. He was, after all, a very learned reader.

'After college, Lord Ainsley was determined to see the world he'd only heard of in books. And with his inheritance and a boat ticket he was off to gain his own fortune. Asia, Middle-East, Africa: to quench the insatiable hunger for anywhere but home.

'This is the time. This was the point and I'm sure of it now. The point when he disappeared.

'In the middle of the Sahara—'

"You have it all wrong, Ms. Rielly."

Lord Ainsley stood over her shoulder like a dark shadow, his black eyes sweeping over her disheveled papers.

She hurriedly covered them with her arms. "Go away, you! These are my memoirs, not yours."

"Hm," he turned to leave, "could have fooled me. Although, as I said, you have it all wrong. So, I suppose you are correct that they aren't mine."

"They aren't!" she declared after him. "Now go stalk someone else, you bother!" Ms. Rielly sighed when he was out of sight, picking up the last page she'd written. "I'd get it right if you'd just tell me instead of leaving it to my fiction."

Ms. Rielly gave the pile a dejected shove and stood from her desk. "Oh, sod it. Why am I here?" She peered out the window to the misty streets of the city below, watching as

13

people gave the mansion a wide berth with hurried steps. She could understand. The Ainsley Manor was a gloomy shadow of its former glory.

An imposing black iron fence surrounded the meager grounds of the estate as the city expanded and encroached toward the property. Not a soul approached the house now that it was darkened by an ever-present cloud of mystery and despair. Rumors flew about the man who had returned quite suddenly home but had not been seen in society since. Suspicions rooted deeply in their minds of the young heir who lived alone in the grand mansion with only his butler and his secrets to accompany him.

Ms. Rielly had heard the same story from any who used to claim knowledge of him before his mysterious return. He'd been such a precocious child, always excitable. Then he had been a successful young man finding his way in the world after tragedy. He had always been amiable and welcoming. Always one to keep his childhood sense of adventure on hand, he was quick to make a witty remark to entertain his guests. Until he returned home from-

"Was it Mumbai?" Ms. Rielly called loudly, glancing at the desk. She rushed to the doorway. "Lord Ainsley! I know you can hear me! Was it India?" She sighed again and leaned against the door frame, tugging habitually at the sleeve of her dress.

"Why am I here?"

Chapter Two
Ms. Rielly and the Lord

'I may not know the whole life story of Lord Ainsley III, but I do know what I have experienced. Including how I met him. And how I came to be in this dismal place called Ainsley Manor.

'I, as the character I've been assigned in the play that is Lord Ainsley's life, must omit certain facts. As even these memoirs could be seen by anyone, it does not bode well for any of us to write the entirety of the events. I suppose that is what one can expect from a private person trying to transcribe their life from bits and pieces. Hopefully, the words will still make sense.

'I came upon Ainsley Manor five months ago for the first time. I sat inside the carriage awaiting my uncle to beckon me forth. Upon his prompt return, what I received was a gruff, unintelligible reply to my perfectly understandable question: "Why are we leaving?"

'As I heard it, a young gentleman of means had been living for quite some time by himself at the manor. Many of the white-gloved, laced ladies of the court had attempted to force an audience with the young man to no avail. Of course, there was one who had long since claimed—ah, but I cannot write of that.

'My uncle was a peacock of a man. Large and oozing prestige, buried long ago under a belly full of whiskey and an expensive coat. However useless he was to society, I held him dear and at the same time clutched at the only connections he could muster from his dusty past of parties and engagements. So, when the good old man mentioned he was once business mates with the family Ainsley, I grasped at the only thread I could.

'An audience was to be had, but the first attempt had us turned away at the door. This did not deter me. If I was to be admitted to any house, it would prove to be the door of Ainsley Manor opening. I would step over that threshold, I swore it.

'My motives were as dark as the history hanging over the Manor. But I assure you, as you may have already deduced, I gained entry. For who else but I could face the challenge of finding a murderer?'

Ms. Rielly paused in her musings to reflect on that day two months ago. She deliberated over whether or not to keep that last segment she'd written. She pulled on her sleeve and bit her lip, gazing off into the memory pooling in her mind.

The day had been cool and the cobblestone slick as Ms. Rielly and her uncle Byron walked up to the wide doors of Ainsley Manor. Byron let the knocker drop twice as Ms. Rielly brushed off her pelisse. An older man in a black waistcoat and short wrist gloves answered and bid them welcome, stepping aside to invite their entry.

"Master Ainsley shall join us shortly in the tea room. I am his butler, Reginald." He gestured to a door. "Please, come this way."

The house was quiet except for the telltale creaks characteristic of an ancient and empty mansion. Ms. Rielly silently marveled at the delicate carvings and detailed architecture revealed in the dim light of lanterns. Not a surface was left untouched or uncovered by oddities the likes of which she'd never seen in person: ivory elephants, glass orbs, tapestries, and photos of a man proudly brandishing a rifle over various corpses of exotic animals.

The tea room was the sparse sore thumb. An ornate stained-glass window tossed reds and blues over a lounging chaise and short tea table. The walls were decorated with pictures of strangers, but otherwise the room bled emptiness. Or, at least, deliberate space. Ms. Rielly noticed her heel sink into an indentation that seemed to have, up until recently, been occupied by a furniture leg.

"Please make yourselves comfortable." Reginald smiled softly. "I shall fetch Master Ainsley."

Ms. Rielly watched the butler's departure contemplatively as Byron threw himself abruptly into the chaise despite its shrieks of protest.

Steam rose from pristine cups filled with the scent of rosehips. The tea had just been poured, as if someone had been sentry to their arrival, and was prepared to perfection. She hooked a finger round the handle and lifted a cup to her lips, breathing in deeply. A noise on the floor above broke her focus and she set the cup down without a sip.

A throat cleared near the doorway and Ms. Rielly turned to fully take in her first sight of Lord Ainsley III. A dapper fellow at first glance but she was certain of one word that described him completely: shade. A creature of shadow and muteness with black pools for eyes and an air of capability about him that swept over Ms. Rielly, disarming her with charm but simultaneously provoking her most primal survival instincts.

Byron shuffled to stand, extending an unreceived hand. "Lord Ainsley. Pleased to see you again. It has been quite some time since—oh, you were just a lad. You would find most difficulty in recognizing me." His niece came forward and he ceased babbling with a small cough. "This is my ward, Ms. Jekyllyne Rielly."

She curtsied. "Pleased to make your acquaintance, Lord Ainsley. Please call me 'Ms. Rielly.'"

To her surprise, Lord Ainsley bowed, taking her dainty hand in his. "Pleased to meet you. I do not receive guests often these days. It is refreshing to hear voices among these rooms again."

"Especially one of a young woman, yes?" Byron gave a hearty laugh, blind to the cold response of both parties.

"My uncle tells me he used to split bonds with your father." Ms. Rielly sat herself. "Something in the more southern investments, if I recall. I hear you too had quite a light foot in lands well over the continents."

Lord Ainsley remained standing even as Byron retreated back to the chaise. "That is correct. I have done much travelling. Although, there is no better cure for light feet than the hearth of your own home."

"Very true, if only you are of the mind that light feet are a disease," she replied.

"And you are not?"

Ms. Rielly tapped her fingernail on the tabletop. "Of what in this home did not light feet supply? Where did you find this treasure?"

She could detect a small corner of his lip curl into a whisper of a smile before he said, "I've enjoyed this immensely, Ms. Rielly. However, I must now request your departure." Without another word, Lord Ainsley vanished into the hall.

Ms. Rielly popped out of her seat in pursuit only to meet with the hands of Reginald. "I do apologize for Master Ainsley. You must excuse him; he is rather busy. Perhaps another day for tea?"

Byron, who had been dozing, awoke with a snort. "Yes, then? All is well." He glanced at his niece's flushed face and the regretful smile of the butler and asked, "Did I muck things up?"

Ms. Rielly could not admit defeat for the day, for on the way out she pleaded use of the loo. Byron proceeded to the carriage with an indistinguishable huff and Reginald directed her to the room deeper within the manor. Then, she took her chance.

Peeking round the door frame, she snuck on silent toes out of the bathroom and down the hall. The flooring was cherry oak on which her heels would betray her position; thus, she held her shoes in hand. She pressed close to the walls, straining to hear should she turn a wrong corner. And when at last she seemed in the clear, footsteps scared her into the nearest room. She held tight to her breath until the steps faded and then looked around to surmise her location.

A study. Much like any other study with a large writing desk and bookshelves instead of wallpaper. There was not a single breath of space to be had and many items were stacked precariously on top of one another. Ms. Rielly feared one misaimed sigh would let loose an avalanche and have her trapped among all sorts of treasures. A dragon buried in its own cave of gold.

This fear soon dissipated as a new wave of curiosity swept over her and took control. She set her shoes down and moved gingerly into the center of the study, noting carefully her placement. The many collections around her did not slow her down; her destination was close and she would not stop.

She reached out to touch the first volume on the shelf behind the desk. It was a heavy volume with a copper tone to its cracked binding. Examining the books more closely, she noticed they were all quite worn. Her finger found a hook at the top of a binding and she pulled, as if to remove it from the shelf.

However, as the book tipped nearly to her grasp, she halted and let it slip back to its former position. With every book she did the same, releasing each with the lift of her finger. One after another her finger plied until she was on tiptoe.

Her fingernails were scratching at the corner of a green binding when Lord Ainsley's voice came from behind her. "Are you fond of novels, Ms. Rielly?"

She abandoned the book slowly, with her back still to him. "You have caught me in the throes of my fondness for them. I apologize for my behavior. I could not help myself when I spied your collection." She turned to face him.

He stood not far, one hand idly twisting among the contents of his desk, his gaze set intently on her. "I understand wholly such passion, as you can see." He motioned to the library.

Ms. Rielly flashed a small smile. "Yes, it is quite a masterpiece, this. I thank you for your hospitality. As well as your forgiveness." She moved toward the door.

Lord Ainsley's arm stretched in front of her face to land on a book. His long fingers lingered there; Ms. Rielly's eyes widened slightly at his proximity. His sleeve brushed her cheek and she breathed in a spicy musk from his hair. He extracted the volume and opened its pages, remaining where he was.

Ms. Rielly carefully and imperceptibly shifted away so she was leaning more into the shelf than toward him. "Lord Ainsley, I—"

"Distracting, aren't they?" he said softly. "You know this one?"

Her eyes darted from the exit to the book's title and then narrowed despite herself. "Yes. I am well familiarized with it."

"Your parents," he continued, "they loved you?"

She smirked behind a hand. "You refer, of course, to my namesake. Yes, there is no question they loved me. Although, they had a queer sense of humor."

"Jekyllyne Rielly. Quite a beautiful rendition of the Jekyll name." Lord Ainsley hefted the book as if weighing it.

"Yes, again a very queer sense of humor." She clenched her teeth but kept her tone casual and friendly. "I notice you have two volumes of that one."

He returned the book to its home. "Yes, one is a first edition." He faced her directly. "I trust you've had the use of the facilities?"

She nodded, remembering her cover. "Yes, thank you."

"Then your uncle shall be waiting. You should not worry him further by your absence." He smiled. "A lady should not be alone long with a gentleman, after all."

"Yes, of course." She grabbed her shoes at the door and stopped. "May I make one generous request of you, Lord Ainsley? Permit me to return. Your library beckons to distract me further."

Lord Ainsley rested his hand on a book high above him. "Yes, you will come again. If only to distract me, Ms. Jekyllyne Rielly."

She did not breathe calmly again until the manor was well out of sight.

Not long after the unsettling events of that day, an invitation to a formal dinner at Ainsley Manor arrived. Byron was filled with unassuming pride, beaming at his ward and declaring the Lord Ainsley quite a catch. Ms. Rielly did not betray her sense of fright: something about that man had made her quite uneasy.

She had heard the stories of Lord Ainsley, of course. But like the origin of her name, the lesser-known truths had not escaped her either. Truths that whispered of disappearances and suspicions.

She thought of this as the manor loomed over her. Reginald greeted them at the doors and once again ushered them inside to the tea room. However, the room had been transformed.

A round ivory table was set in the nook of windows with a crystal set of tea ware sparkling atop its smooth finish. A gorgeous set of lush velvet chairs flanked a complete chess board, the pieces carved from stone and poised for battle. Botticelli and Monet dressed the walls and a large tiger skin yawned toothily from the floor. Mounds of books were stacked wherever space permitted. Where the room had once been cold and empty, now it was full of life. Textures and colors played joyfully through the room and warmth spread from the hearth filled with logs that crackled contentedly. Such a stark contrast from before, the room brimmed with myriads of beautiful and enchanting details.

And upon a cursory inspection, not a volume of Ms. Rielly's namesake was to be found.

It was as if she had opened the door to a dream. All the items stirred her deeply and her mind hummed with inspiration. She was quite enchanted by everything around her by the time music floated to her ears.

"Johann Sebastian." She closed her eyes. "And what is that smell?"

"Your tea." Lord Ainsley appeared alongside Reginald. "Imported from China. I hope it will be to your liking." He pulled out a chair and she accepted the seat. This time, he joined her.

"I'll chase away the chill by the fire, if you don't mind," Byron said, falling back into the chaise with which he was beginning to become intimately acquainted.

Lord Ainsley held up a hand, signaling Reginald. "Tend to the menu. See that it is prepared for us by six."

"Yes, Master Ainsley." Reginald left them, closing the door quietly.

Ms. Rielly tried and failed not to smile. "What is all this?"

"I felt that I had not achieved the proper title of host in my previous dealings with you. I only wish to amend that slight and treat you as the guest you are," he said without a blink of hesitation.

She shook her head. "But this… no, this is more than is necessary. This is more than being a proper host, Lord Ainsley. If I may say so, it is as if you have peered into my innermost thoughts and procured the result before my very eyes. How did you know I favored *Venus*?"

"*Venus* is a masterful artwork that any human being would be enamored with," he remarked simply. "And as to the rest, I feel as if we may be two souls of similar inclinations. I believe that you enjoy, as I do, to be surrounded by intellectually and visually stimulating treasures. You would not feel at home unless that need was satisfied."

"You continue to shock me, Lord Ainsley." She brought a cup to her lips and let the taste of Asia sweep over her tongue. She sipped slowly, allowing herself this moment to rein in her senses before they were lost to her completely. The tea was sweet with a sharp bite, reminding her of her bitter mission.

Any other woman would have been felled before such an intoxicating man. His black eyes glinted mischievously, reflecting the light of the fire. An enticing scent drifted from his collar. He was impeccably dressed and held himself in such a manner that no amount of amusing surroundings could demand attention as his presence did. Again Ms. Rielly could feel herself being lulled into the trap around him, one from which she was certain she would never escape should she succumb.

However, the bitter tea and the dark motive within her brought her back from the brink.

She set the cup down. "Such a lot of distractions. Seems almost as if you never intended us to make it to dinner. Why, we could spend lifetimes forgetting ourselves just in this room."

Lord Ainsley smiled a little. "So I've overdone it. Do forgive me. I am not yet accustomed to having guests again."

"Perhaps we can change that," Ms. Rielly suggested. "I happen to be adept at teaching."

"And I at learning."

Reginald soon led them all to the dining room where a feast of venison and potatoes waited. A course of various fruits and crisp French beans followed. The wine was red and partnered with a milky brie on sectioned baguette. The selection as a whole reflected the distinct status the Ainsley family had maintained over the years.

Byron leaned back in his chair, setting off a chorus of groans from the tired wood. "You surely know how to accommodate guests, Lord Ainsley!"

"When the occasion calls for it," he said, looking at Ms. Rielly. She smiled but didn't meet his eyes.

"I do hope this can mark the beginning of many dinners." Byron raised an eyebrow. "And perhaps a partnership?"

"A conversation for another time," Lord Ainsley said. "We should not talk business in front of the lady."

"Oh, my boy," he chastised. "Not that kind of—"

"Ms. Rielly, are you well?"

She pressed a hand to her chest. "I am afraid I am not. I feel quite disoriented. Perhaps if I wet my face a bit." She stood to make for the restroom but, in stepping away from her chair, swooned.

Lord Ainsley was at her side before Byron could react, steadying her weakened legs. "Reginald, prepare two rooms. Ms. Rielly and her uncle will be staying tonight. Summon the doctor immediately."

Byron was nodding but Ms. Rielly shook her head. "No, Lord Ainsley. We shan't inconvenience you. You have already been most gracious." Her brow furrowed and had a light sheen to it.

"Nonsense," he reassured her. "The journey is long and rough for you. Allow my doctor to tend to you tonight and aid your recovery for your return home on the morrow. A gracious host would not think of letting you leave in this state."

Reginald spoke up, "The rooms are ready. The doctor shall be here within the hour."

"Very good." Lord Ainsley guided her out. "You shall stay here tonight. My doctor shall ensure you are well by morning."

Ms. Rielly conceded and was introduced to a quaint bedroom on the second floor. The windows were heavily covered with dark curtains; the bed was soft with goose down and draped with an ornamented canopy. There was a small fireplace already lit and a washing bowl on the bureau.

"Reginald has left night clothing for you on the bed and the doctor will be here presently." Upon her assurances she would be quite well, Lord Ainsley left the room.

Ms. Rielly breathed in deeply and steeled herself. She changed into the nightgown provided and tried not to tug nervously at the sleeve while she awaited the doctor's arrival.

He was a stout man with practiced fingers and old eyes. He performed his poking and prodding with the expected bedside manner and diagnosed her with a stomach ailment. This was to be cured with rest and fluids.

He smiled as he gathered his bag. "You shall be right in the morning. Do not place undue stress upon your body."

"Yes, Sir," Ms. Rielly agreed. "I shall do as you recommend."

He chuckled a little. "Been quite some time since I've been called here. I didn't expect to find another young lady receiving my care."

Ms. Rielly's heart jumped. "Another lady? Do you recall her name? When was she here?"

"Calm, now." The doctor laughed. "Oh, it was so long ago. Now you rest and hydrate, my dear." He went to the door and paused, saying one last thing before he departed. "Perhaps this is good for him."

Ms. Rielly could feel herself getting closer to pulling back the shroud hanging over the house of Ainsley. She peered at herself in a mirror along the wall and studied the woman who studied her back. Mousy features and sharp cheeks, brown curls gathered carefully atop her head, and freckles dotting her nose. Small lips set in a grim line and eyes smoldering with renewed determination. The night was unfolding exactly as she had hoped.

Chapter Three

Lord Ainsley and the Lady

Nightfall had descended on Ainsley Manor, but the windows were lit with movement and merriment. Voices congregated and could be heard dispelling any quiet with laughter. The house was open and people celebrated. Men in coats served champagne and hors d'oeuvres; women twirled in brightly colored party dresses and white gloves. Music captured and carried the guests with finely tuned notes and boisterous overtures.

Conversations tittered with compliments on the food, the attendants, and most of all the master of the house who had just returned home from another far-off adventure. The Lord's eyes were bright and youthful, his posture not yet weighed down by too many years of experience. Another young man whispered every so often in his ear, smiling wickedly and eyeing the girls. Lord Ainsley would laugh and playfully push his friend, with his own gaze focused on similar subjects. Men in fancy tailcoats approached, speaking words of business and the future.

Once the men moved on, Ainsley's friend wrapped an arm around his shoulder. "Oh, great Lord Ainsley. Permit us to kiss your rear just a little more!"

"Silence, you devil." Ainsley chuckled. "They are just trying to enterprise—"

"Expand horizons! Do what has never been done before!" The other boy sighed. "I've heard your campaign many a time, your lordship—"

"Alan!" A young girl parted the crowd and fell into the arms of Ainsley's friend. "I haven't seen you for ages!"

"Always one for exaggeration." Alan released the girl. "May I present my cousin, Miss Jane Peighton. Jane, this is Ben Ainsley."

"Benjamin." He took her hand and kissed it lightly. "'Ben' is Alan's pet name for me." He elbowed Alan.

"Pleased to meet you." She pulled her hand back and turned to Alan. "I have heard quite a lot of you from my cousin's correspondence. Which has dwindled as of late!"

"It really has not been that long!" Alan protested. "Jane demands letters monthly, but by the time they arrive, her patience has run out. Her fault, however, lies in the fact that she practices her studies in America."

"I've not yet travelled abroad that way." Ainsley smiled winningly. "Not yet."

His friend chuckled. "Ben is quite the entrepreneur and explorer. America might be too dull for you." Alan clapped him on the back.

Jane eyed Ainsley, seeming to finally acknowledge him. "Yes, I have heard of your dragging Alan all over God's creation. I personally value men who are much less unsettled." She focused back on her cousin, ready to dismiss Ainsley.

He spoke up, shocking her. "And men tend to favor women who don't mind a little spontaneity. Or a challenge."

Jane sighed. "If I saw a challenge, I would rise to meet it, Benjamin Ainsley. And as for spontaneity, a woman such as I need not such instability. However, that does not mean my life lacks excitement."

"I would not dream of assuming anything of your life, Miss Peighton," Ainsley said. "Perhaps you could allow the same for me? More time may alter both of our first impressions."

She contemplated for a moment. "More time may be afforded. I shall be staying at Forrinsworth for a fortnight. Perhaps in that time you would demonstrate your much-practiced spontaneity." She bid them both good night and melded back into the throng.

"Did my cousin just invite you to her estate?" Alan stared after her.

"Curious behavior from one who seems to find me intolerable."

"Yes, 'unstable' was her word," Alan said. "And not a challenge, I believe. She detests you!"

Ainsley smiled. "Yes. Yes, she does."

Forrinsworth was a cobblestone country beauty. The cottage was nearly a day's ride from any bustling city streets and gloomy weather. The sun was bright on the sprawling meadows and highlighted the dust kicked up from the horses on the uneven roads. The carriage bearing Ainsley and Madam Tusor rocked violently at times, immediately setting off aggravated sighs from the older occupant.

Madam Tusor was a plump woman with a sharp tongue and quick mind. Her face was a bit mottled with the heat and her bun was slowly deflating, but she did not complain. Ainsley liked her for this. The madam was a free spirit with the reins of her life firmly gripped within her own hands. She always told the truth and yet never offended him in the slightest way. She maintained a smart wit and keen protective instinct for the former recipient of her care. When once she had been the child Ainsley's governess, now she was a long-time confidant and business counselor.

Madam Tusor folded her hands into her lap. "The Peightons are a difficult family to deal with, Benjamin. You understand how this may look: a gentleman calling on a young girl. Does she know you are not there for her?"

Ainsley gave her a brief look. "She won't care a bit. She despises me."

"And yet, she invited you here in such a brazen way. She seems to receive what she wants as often as she demands." Madam Tusor coughed a little, some dust inevitably finding its way into the coach. "Miss Peighton's mother is to thank for that. And for this ride today. After her husband's death, she quickly ran off with another man. American, too. It was the scandal of the year. But, of course, you've already done your research on their benefactor. Thank God they married before having their son. Jane is the daughter of the late Lord Hannes. Poor man died too soon. Cancer of the jaw."

"I know very well their background, Madam. Alan does have loose lips." Ainsley twirled a lock of hair by his ear. "But if I must take advantage of the product of scandals, I shall do so. But ever with precaution, as you taught me, Lorri."

She laughed at the use of her nickname. "You are twisting your hair just as you used to when you were small.

32

You have nothing over which to twist your hair about, my dear. You are a brilliant strategist and all will go well."

His fingers stopped. "And you are ever as wise to the future, Lorri. Tell me, why did a girl who most definitely loathes me invite me here?"

Madam Tusor smiled warmly. "Dear boy, it has been quite some time since this woman could decipher a young girl's heart. Remembering my own, I can only warn you. When one moment my heart beat as calm as the seas, the next it would tear asunder any unfortunate to be caught in them. Some girls are as I was: predictably unpredictable. Others are simple little dolls with empty skulls." She noticed his face become puzzled. "I give you this advice when it comes to girls: treat them as the fragile dolls they are, but always remember what may lie beneath their painted faces. Do you understand, Benjamin?"

Ainsley nodded and returned her smile. "Yes, Madam."

The cottage came into sight just as the coach rounded some trees. The carriage stopped in front of the door and they were greeted by the housekeeper as they descended. She was a tall woman with severe features and bony hands. She welcomed them and introduced herself as Mrs. Addison.

"The lady is upstairs and shall be with you presently," she said, leading them to the sitting room. She had a placid smile and practiced tone.

"May we enquire as to when the master of the house shall be joining us?" Madam Tusor asked with a similar but more genial tone.

"Oh, yes," Mrs. Addison said. "The Lord Peighton is away on business." She left abruptly.

Ainsley could see the edge now in Madam Tusor's eyes that gave away her inner irritation. Had they been elsewhere he was sure she would have commented on the housekeeper's impertinence and disrespect. He could see the angry thoughts buzzing around her, most likely about how John Peighton was hardly a lord at all and how this was no way to treat an actual lord. Not being home to receive guests! And what an affected housekeeper. Probably American too, with that horrible accent!

Yet, all these thoughts were hidden behind a peaceful, passive façade. Madam Tusor and Ainsley could always trust on being themselves around each other. She was an invaluable companion, always able to evaluate a person accurately at first glance and never steering him wrong. But as they were in foreign territory, Madam Tusor sat straight and buried truth behind her eyes, her cheeks rosy and nothing amiss. This was another reason Ainsley liked her.

"Good day, Lord Ainsley, Madam Tusor. Welcome to our humble Forrinsworth." A woman's voice drew their attention. She was a beautifully proportioned woman with tiny hands and kind blue eyes framed by dark yellow hair. Her skin was fair and cheeks slightly freckled, laugh lines left behind from overuse around her full lips. "I am Ailsa Peighton, Lady of Forrinsworth. Please make yourselves at home."

"Pleased to meet you, Lady Peighton." Ainsley stepped forward to kiss her hand.

Her cheeks reddened. "A custom from another land?" Her laugh was as musical chimes.

"I apologize for the habits he has picked up. Lord Ainsley forgets often which country he is in. I am Madam Lorraine Tusor." She smiled gracefully.

"Mum!" Jane descended the stairs and joined them. She wore an understated dress of blue with black ribbon tied at the sleeves. "You've met Benjamin Ainsley. I am glad to see you have arrived in good time." She ignored the madam.

"Shall we go for a walk then?" Lady Peighton asked. "Such a lovely day should not pass unaccompanied."

After agreeable consent, the party moved outside to languidly enjoy the day and its splendor. They strolled among recently trimmed rose bushes, chatting idly about unimportant topics and letting the breeze carry the words away. For a time, the group remained uninterrupted until a maid appeared.

"Dinner shall be ready soon, my lady," she said with a small nod.

Lady Peighton thanked her. "I had best go inspect the menu. Madam, you would honor me with your presence. My maid will stay with Jane should she need anything."

Madam Tusor's eyes flashed briefly, only communicating covertly to Ainsley. Her painted lips never quivered as she and the lady left the three in the field. The maid was quiet as a mouse and made herself scarce as she trailed behind them. There was no doubt what she was truly there for.

"My mother was glad when she heard I had finally extended a palm branch to someone." Jane chuckled. "You have probably realized I am not much of a people person."

"People persons may not always be as pleasing as they think. I find them quite full of themselves," Ainsley said.

Her eyelashes fluttered but she remained stiff-necked. "You seem very talented at turning everything into a compliment for the ladies."

"And you at deflecting such compliments." He caught himself ready to insult her. "I apologize. I did not come to cause you further slights."

"I see no slight, Benjamin Ainsley. Only a challenge." Now she smiled at him. Her expression changed. "Where is Susan?"

They surveyed the field, but the maid was nowhere to be seen.

"Perhaps we should head back?" Ainsley motioned to the house.

"Are you uncomfortable being alone with a harmless lady, Lord Ainsley?" Jane made a serious mocking pout. "Are you afraid I shall take advantage of you? Or worried about the scene being improper?"

"I only think of your reputation," he replied.

"Oh!" she sighed dramatically. "If only we were truly alone, Lord Ainsley, and did not have the whole of society upon our backs! Maybe then we could be ourselves."

Ainsley took pause, gauging her. "It is hard to remember society's presence around you, Jane Peighton. Shall we toss off our yoke?" He tested her response carefully, as if testing the waters for dangerous degrees of temperature. Would his face unmasked shock her with its coldness? Would her face melt to reveal a monstrosity or hidden beauty?

Jane's eyes were muddied with conflicting feelings. She studied him as if waiting for the very thing he did. The paint began to crack and chip, falling away with a sigh of release.

She presented herself, arms out wide and lips pulled back in a grin. "I knew you were the same as I!"

Benjamin relaxed. "The same?"

She loosened the ribbons from her sleeves, pulling them out. "Oh, yes. Such a charming man was the one I met at the party. Such a copy of all the other men. Such a heart breaker. But you could not fool me for long, dear Benjamin. No, not a kindred spirit such as I!"

Her whole demeanor had shifted, as if another person entirely had stepped forward from within her. This personality skipped and teased flowers with her fingertips, her inner self free to roam. She tied her hair back with the previously abandoned ribbons and raced off with Benjamin now hooked and following behind her.

Gone was the jaded, barbed girl. Gone was Lord Ainsley. Soon they were deep in the wood by the road and lost to each other's true guises.

Benjamin threw off his coat. "You believed me haughty?"

"You appeared so. Just as you had rehearsed, no doubt." Jane was high in a tree, her feet dangling with her shoes long gone. "As I had rehearsed my own snooty performance. But I could sense there was more to you. Underneath, there would be a brooding and more satirical persona."

"You could not have possibly known for sure." He balanced on a nearby rock. "Is that why you had me here? To divide my defenses and discover for yourself?"

"I believe you figured out my plan before I had for myself." She kicked her legs out and dropped to her feet. "You were simple from the start. You couldn't help but insult me every chance your true self could slip through. It is as if you were begging for someone to attempt to tear through your walls and discover them secretly made of paper."

"Yes, you did well in baiting me. It was strange how easily I lost control of myself." He shook his head in disbelief.

Jane had been forthright and excited until then, but she suddenly was calm and stern. "Tell me now. You did not come to placate my request or to discover my inner self. You did not come to knock at my walls to discover them to be weak or strong. You came to employ John Peighton."

Ainsley was stoic. "Yes, that is the truth. You read me as if I am pages of words written plainly before you. I came to ask John Peighton for funding and a key. The key to opening the door to America."

"What for?" Jane tilted her head to the side. "America holds nothing new for explorers."

He took in a slow, deep breath. "I do not intend to explore it. I intend to use it to achieve my true self's desire. My dearest dream."

She waited without judgment and with an open mind. She waited until Benjamin could be sure she would not respond with pity or laughter. Yes, she waited weeks in fact for him to finally reveal to her his dream.

A ruffled Madam Tusor found them wandering near the flowers and chastised them sweetly for being unchaperoned. Jane later told him that she had ordered the maid to discreetly "forget" her duties. Lady Peighton entertained her guests with fine food and niceties, bidding them a safe journey home and offering an open door whenever they so desired. She apologized for the master's absence and assured them that their continued friendship would present opportunities to meet the elusive man.

On the carriage ride home, Madam Tusor questioned Ainsley very little, trusting that he would have taken measures had he been wary of being left unattended. She listened as he told her of his enlightening evening, only making occasional noises to assure him she still listened. Then he stopped and gazed off into his short-term memory, reliving all he had just described.

"I've never before felt so bare and yet so unfettered," he said in innocent wonder. "What is this that has rendered me so?"

Madam Tusor smiled. "I have never in my years of watching you grow seen you like this, Benjamin Ainsley. All I can say to you is that this Miss Jane Peighton must be one remarkable young lady."

"Yes," Ainsley concurred. "She is and could very well be... the lady."

Chapter Four

Once Fooled, Shame on You
Twice Fooled...

"What did he say?" Jane's excitement could barely be contained. "What did John say?!" She never referred to her step-father by anything but his name.

In repeated visits and many more private talks, Ainsley had come to know of Jane's disdain for her mother's sudden elopement. In truth, she did not understand how her mother could have been swept out of grief and into love so soon after her father's passing.

Not long after making Lord Ainsley's acquaintance, she took advantage of her second home to escape to America. She valued the customs and changes she experienced there and bore not even a hint of ill-will toward the product of the affair: her baby brother Michael. She often doted on him, writing in letters to Ainsley of how he had grown and how he loved to be tickled.

After many letters tossed to and fro over continents, Jane at last returned to Forrinsworth. Now she and Benjamin sat at their favorite tree and caught up aimlessly.

"John and I have yet to conclude our dealings," Ainsley replied.

"You mean you haven't told him yet?" Jane let out an exasperated sigh. "Benjamin, you might as well burn your reels if you're not going to use them! What of your dream? You can't just—ugh, this is too frustrating."

Benjamin laughed. "Now, now. Don't get tongue-tied after all of this."

She breathed in and centered herself. "Benny. Benjamin. You have a gift. You can give the world to others. Please, don't let this dream escape you now that you have the means to achieve it!"

She reached into a fold of her skirt and gave him something thin and rolled. "Do this for me and yourself. The only way I'll ever see as you do is if you do as your dream demands: make your stories real. Turn the printed book, the captured memories, into images. Moving pictures."

***

Lord Ainsley gazed at the scrap of movie reel in his hands, still hearing Jane's words echoing down through time. Down to the night Ms. Rielly slept in his guestroom. He tucked the old reel between the pages of a book in his study and muttered aloud the lady's words: "Moving pictures."

Ms. Rielly awoke from her light slumber in the middle of the night. She rose from the bed and let the cool stillness calm her. Now she could put her plan into action, uninhibited by the anxiety of being caught. She had waited long enough that her host and his butler would surely be asleep and out of the way.

Ms. Rielly padded barefoot down the halls she had memorized earlier to the room she desired. The door to Lord Ainsley's study barely whispered as she entered, as if it too were holding its breath. Moonlight refracted off glass instruments and golden pens. She reached at last for the volume that had narrowly avoided her previously: the first edition of *Dr. Jekyll and Mr. Hyde.*

The book was attached heavily to the case and with a swift pull, it gave a jarring clank. The entire bookshelf shifted and popped out with a hiss of air. It swung open on hidden hinges, allowing just enough space for her to move through. Beyond the entrance lay a tight passage of stone steps leading down into the damp unknown. Deeper still, a small light beckoned.

Ms. Rielly descended with care, one hand skimming a wall and her eyesight adjusting slowly. The atmosphere was tepid and ancient, but the stairs were well maintained. The light grew closer, but she could not discern the origin. The passage spread out into an overwhelming nothingness. The ground now creaked, hard wood beneath her feet. She could just make out the curving path of wooden planks that circled the room followed by railings. She gripped the closest one, anonymous items littering the space around her and collecting at the sides.

Finally, she made her way to the nearest object, one hand still on the railing and the other pulling at a rough cloth. The material slipped into a pile at her toes and she blinked at the figure in front of her. She almost laughed, realizing she stared at herself reflected in a mirror on easel legs.

She went to the next object and yanked again at the dusty coverlet. She coughed at the air she stirred up and puzzled over the large projector left in disuse and neglect. Ms. Rielly touched it gently and the cold metal stole the heat from her fingertips. She shivered and continued.

Behind the mirror was a table with multiple articles strewn across it. Glasses with shattered lenses, bottles with slanted script, hammers and nails. Most confusing of all were the hair pieces, the feathers and furs, and lastly a small tube of lipstick. Ms. Rielly picked this last item up and closed her fist around it.

Something clattered and she gasped, whipping around. There was no movement, only silence. Her breath had quickened, a claustrophobic feeling gnawing at her sides. Her distressed search landed frantically on another bulky lump in the dark and she clawed at the sackcloth.

She screamed and recoiled from the body that hung there: its face twisted in a monstrous sneer, its eyes wide in the throes of fear. She crashed into the mirror and it shattered as it struck the ground. The light source found where the mirror lay and bounced off in a million reflected bursts.

Ms. Rielly backed into something thick and screamed at the animal poised there, its sharp jaws open wide with a roar. She ran, the wood under her groaning, colliding into ropes that dangled. She was struggling to free herself when something big swung out to hit her, its wings flapping. Her ankle caught and Ms. Rielly tumbled, the railing cracking and giving way.

Strong arms wrapped around her waist and stopped her from falling to meet the unforgiving ground below. She saw a glimpse of Lord Ainsley before she fainted.

When she awoke, the cavern had been transformed. Lanterns were lit intermittently and revealed the nightmares she had battled. The body of the panicked man was a robed mannequin with an empty eyed droopy mask. The animal was a taxidermy mountain cat with a glossy stare and yellowed fangs. A model bi-plane with broken wings was swinging nearby, the victim of her flailing. The rest of the room held similar oddities of hats and costumes, masks and accoutrements, sets and contraptions.

Ms. Rielly sat up from a mattress filled with hay. Lord Ainsley stood with his back to her, tending the projector. "What is all this?"

"A life's work," came his soft voice. "Most likely not what you were expecting to find. So, what were you after, Ms. Rielly?" He turned to her.

She stood and held up the lipstick she still had in her possession. "Just another prop? The initials on the bottom prove its owner. Now where is she, Lord Ainsley? Where have you hidden her body?"

Lord Ainsley had moved the projector to a table in the middle of the room, where the wood sloped down to meet stone. He didn't move as Ms. Rielly circled him cautiously, her tiny frame hardened and poised to strike. She kept the table and a few feet of distance between them for a protective barrier.

"Is this where you've kept her? Did you kill her quickly or keep her alive for a time?"

Lord Ainsley remained unperturbed by her line of inquisition. "Of whom do you speak, Ms. Rielly? Perhaps you have hit your head. Or you are still feeling out of sorts from dinner? All this disturbance and fright, I wouldn't be surprised. Nor would anyone else."

She flexed a hand at her side. "This lipstick is proof she was here. That is enough for Scotland Yard. They'll be crawling all over your peculiar laboratory to destroy your façade, the truth wrung from your evil core! My uncle is upstairs, you will not get away with murdering me, as you did her!"

Lord Ainsley laughed, loudly and eerily in the open space. "Ms. Rielly, junior detective. Running rampant through London's crime-soaked streets in her petticoat and heels. Solving mysteries even a great detective would tip his hat to." His smile seemed out of place.

"Don't toy with me. I am not a defenseless little girl!" She reached into the long sleeve of her nightgown and gasped, the backup plan she'd had no longer there.

"Do you think I wouldn't notice you were armed? Although, I am not sure that you can classify that as a weapon." He tasked her. "You haven't done enough research, Ms. Rielly. I, however, have." He tinkered with the work on his table, no longer paying her any mind. "Jekyllyne Victoria Rielly. Parents deceased. House fire when you were six. Your nouveau riche Uncle Byron spirits you into his care and enrolls you in St. Mary's where you stayed mostly to yourself. You studied diligently and by the time you reached adulthood, realized you were different than other girls."

"Enough," Ms. Rielly warned.

He went on, "Your affinity for science, although not altogether distasteful, is quite frowned upon by society. Nonetheless, you are a woman determined and went off to college to excel in biology. Your love for the profession grew, but no one would employ you. Without an outlet, you ran your own experiments…"

"Stop it!" She ran at him.

He whirled on her, swiftly trapping her between the table and his arms. She sucked in air to scream but caught a glint in the corner of her vision that made her voice choke back. The scream dried up inside her lungs and the room seemed to tilt.

"This is yours." Lord Ainsley tapped the silver scalpel against her neck. "Was this the one you used in your first dissection?"

"No," she said shakily. "This one was." He felt a hard jab in his side to emphasize her threat. "You didn't think I had more than one?"

Suddenly he smiled, his eyes shimmering with pride. "We are kindred spirits. I could use someone like you, Ms. Jekyllyne Rielly."

"What?" Her voice came out high pitched.

"You are as sharp as your scalpels and I need someone not afraid to venture into dangerous places." He lowered the knife.

Ms. Rielly couldn't help but feel puzzled. "You are a murderer. You think I am to aid you in any way?"

"I have not murdered anyone, Ms. Rielly. Definitely not the owner of that lipstick." He sighed. "Those initials? Do they match the alleged victim of your imagination?"

"Of course it matches. It stands for Moira Annabel—" she stopped, staring again at the tiny letters.

"Perhaps it reads 'M.L.T.' She always put the 'M' on everything, even though it stood for 'Madam.' Now if you are finished with your accusations, we could begin the so-called paperwork." He placed a gentle hand on hers. "Might you lower your sword?"

The knife stayed. "Before. You had said you need a person. Explain."

"Yes, I do my research, Ms. Rielly." His hand slipped closer to the scalpel. "I have some goals in mind that involve someone of your distinct abilities and discretion. So, I rekindled my old connections and contacted your uncle."

"You were pulling the strings from the beginning! From the start, you knew I would come here and why." She shook her head, grimacing at her own ineptitude.

"Yes, I had already noted the connection between you and a missing girl. A friend from your previous school. However, I didn't expect you to aim your investigation at me. Coincidence can be mysterious that way."

He let her think for a minute and collect her conclusions. "Now, Ms. Jekyllyne Rielly, will you keep my secret if I keep yours?"

"That depends on the goals you mentioned. What would I be helping you with? And what would I get out of it?"

Lord Ainsley smiled. "First, you'll write. And then, using your talents and mine together, we shall uncover the answers we have both been seeking."

"Well, that could mean anything!" She threw her hands up in frustration and Lord Ainsley gasped, the scalpel nicking his finger. "Oh! I am sorry! I didn't mean to!" Ms. Rielly grabbed his wrist to place pressure on the wound, only to gape in shock. "Your blood! Your blood is black!"

Lord Ainsley pulled away and wrapped a kerchief around the oozing cut. "Like I had said, answers we both have been seeking. I will help you find your friend. You, in time, will help me unravel the secrets of this strange affliction. Does this sound like an equal exchange?"

Ms. Rielly nodded somberly. "Yes. As long as you hold up your end, I will do all I can to find out what is wrong with your blood."

"In time," he repeated. "Just one last stipulation: you will not question me and you will live here. I will arrange things with your uncle so that this is understandable."

Thus, Ms. Rielly took up residency in Ainsley Manor. She began to write what she believed would pass as Lord Ainsley's memoirs, squeezing out as much information of his exploits as she could without questioning him. After some time of finding nothing to do, she began to write idly about her own duties to chase away the boredom. Lord Ainsley barely spoke to her at all except to demand patience and remind her of her promise. His threatening tones did not, however, quell her habit to obsess and talk and talk and talk.

They lived with carefully set boundaries. An invisible understanding filled the space between them. They silently acknowledged the mutual distrust and comradery, realizing that they both had questions going unanswered. Lord Ainsley knew Ms. Rielly did not fully believe him innocent in her friend's disappearance, but she would keep her scalpels sharpened and on her person until she found the truth she was certain he could provide. She knew that the lord held more cards in his hands than he may have thought, with the quest for her friend not being the only thing keeping her there. She quelled the growing desire inside her to study his blood closely; her passion for biology almost unbearable. What discoveries hid within him and his blood?

Despite the general distrust born of strangers living together, they also detected an unspoken agreement between them. They never spoke of their varying and queer hobbies, him with his decaying collection of props and her with her fondness for anatomical queries that she practiced on unfortunate birds. But this nonconformity they shared drew them into an unlikely partnership.

Ms. Rielly began to feel her long-lasting suffering dwindling however, and she soon was wandering the halls of the manor as if lost. Lord Ainsley could feel her staring from corners, practically radiating worry. He knew she would snap soon, but he told her to wait. When she would finally give in and demand why and for what they waited, he would permit her one answer.

"Wait for the streets to become wet."

Chapter Five

'Souls of the Lost Are Compelled to Walk Its Streets.'
William Butler Yeats

'I have never met someone so whole and yet incomplete at the same time. Lord Ainsley vexes me more as time passes. As I approach solving one of the riddles surrounding him, another takes its place and I am sent into a tailspin.

'I write to my uncle to assure him of my guarded honor and safety. To the outside world, I may pass as a maid or perhaps a scribe. No matter, for who in the streets of London pays attention to another absent girl?

'My mind wanders, as it does every day, back to her. Was this how it began? Slowly but surely, her memory fading and all evidence of her having lived gone? Am I the only one who didn't forget her? The only one who remembers her for more than what she had become?

'After I had returned from college, I saw her. Though the years had altered us both, I knew it was her. In some of my more backdoor dealings with undertakers, I had found her.

'She wrapped a shawl around her bare and freckled shoulders against the bite of London air, her lips bruised red and stockings torn. She saw but brushed me off, turning to more promising enquiries. She eyed me suspiciously with her peripheral, going about her business.

'"Moira." I saw her start at the use of her name. "It's Jekyllyne Rielly. From early school. Moira, how did you get here?"

'She swore at me, trying to frighten me away. She hissed under her breath for me to leave, insisting that I had mistaken her for someone else. Then a man in a dark coat and hat took her arm and led her down the corridor.

'I remember tugging at my sleeve, reassuring myself of where I had hidden my scalpel. I left, but returned several more times to speak to her. She would always ignore me, sometimes pushing me away or leaving her post early. At times I would stay with her until well into the night and just talk when there was no one else around. I'd tell her of my life and what had become of me. I confessed to her my darkest secrets, as she had had no choice when I discovered hers. For a while, I believed she didn't even listen.

'But she did.

'One night, I was feeling quite low in spirits. I was contemplating the world around me and how I fit into the picture. I was shaken, not sure where I would go in life if I could not follow my passion. I looked up and suddenly found her staring at me.

'"There's room for all of us in this world," she said.

'I was too shocked to engage her in further conversation that night. I returned the next, eager to hear if she would speak again, but she was gone. I searched all her usual spots

51

and even inquired of her to some familiar faces, but no one had seen her. The fog of London had swept through and swallowed her up. It surrendered to me only one thing: Moira's shawl.

'Then I had heard of a young woman disappearing into a manor and never coming out. Reflecting now, it was most likely a rumor fed by haunting stories and conspiratorial tendencies. Besides, no one said how old the story was. It mattered not to me; I was tirelessly looking for answers and had finally seen some light. And now I am here, sure in my feeling that even if Lord Ainsley did not dispatch her himself, he certainly has the power and influence to find out who did. And if he did kill her and deceive me, then my scalpels shall study him.

'Black! Black as the ink on this page. He won't divulge any information he may already have yet, but I am keen to find out! He shall have to tell me eventually, as it is why he brought me here. Why else seek the employ of a person such as me? Moira was right in her words: the world has found me a small place in which I fit.'

Ms. Rielly reread her writings, pondering the time that had passed since she first moved in. Much had changed. She felt less naïve and slept with scalpel close.

That very day, she planned to go to Lord Ainsley and demand, at least, a vial of his blood. If she had to wait, she would work as she did so and begin diagnosis. She relied heavily on the notion that his need of her was even a mote stronger than her need for him, but she knew she was bluffing to herself and could do nothing to force his hand. She once again hoped that he would not realize that he held all the cards. He held the power to finding Moira and although she made it seem she would be doing him a favor, she was truly captivated by his unusual blood.

She went into his study and slammed her hands down on the desk. He had been sitting reading a newspaper, which he lowered. She dramatically glared at him. "No more waiting. I'm beginning to think you called me here just to have a woman's presence in the house. I shall wait no longer, I say. You will give—"

"The paper."

"What?" Her voice squeaked.

"Underneath your poor, chipped nails, dear Ms. Rielly, lies today's Chronicle." He motioned with a nod. "Please read aloud the headline."

She craned her neck sideways to see properly and read: "'Torso-Killer or Jack the Ripper? Body Found at Whitehall.'" She looked up. "What is the weight of this to me?"

"The streets of London have at last become wet again. Wet with a certain crime for which we have both been awaiting. This is our starting point, Ms. Rielly. It was only a matter of time." Lord Ainsley levelled his gaze seriously. "This is where we shall find your answers. And perhaps your friend."

Ms. Rielly lifted the paper and studied the article. "So we are to go to Whitehall?"

"Yes, but first..." He dredged the piles of his desk and handed her a slip of paper.

She gasped. "Is this a medical license?"

"You will need it for where we are going. Also, you might as well have one; you are capable enough." He scoffed at her disbelief. "Creating a manipulated license is not a task that should cause such awe."

"It is illegal."

"So are many of the tasks ahead of us, but the law does not find solutions for obvious reasons." He sighed. "Do not tell me you can haggle with shady morticians, but forgery is beneath you?"

Ms. Rielly huffed. "Right, then! But what are we to do at Whitehall? They've recovered remains and are engaging in their own investigation. Scotland Yard is already taking care of this."

"Correct. That is where we shall go," Lord Ainsley stood, grabbing his heavy coat and making for the door.

"To Scotland Yard?" She chased after him. "But, Lord Ainsley! It's Scotland Yard!"

Chief Inspector Henry John Swanson was a gruff man with a large mustache and a crisp uniform. He was standoffish and loud, with a drive for justice and a habit of rambling. Just the man to suit Lord Ainsley's needs.

Swanson was quick to notice the strangers in his domain. "And who is this? Who let them in? If you're from the papers, I'll have you locked up with the bloody drunkards!"

The crime scene was located at a fair distance from where a slew of officers with foul moods surrounded the entrance to a construction site. The hour was late and yet curious citizens gathered to whisper and speculate. Ms. Rielly could only imagine the problems the bureau would be having in trying to keep the city's confidence in them. A body found in the future location of Scotland Yard itself was quite a blemish on their record.

"This is an outrage!" Swanson came at Lord Ainsley aggressively. Ms. Rielly fully expected the man to deck Ainsley but he stopped short, finally spying the credentials flashed from the Lord's hand. He straightened and saluted. "Apologies, sir. We have been hard pressed to contain this one. Holding down the line has made everyone tense."

Lord Ainsley stuffed the identification away too soon for Ms. Rielly to glimpse. "Quite understandable, Chief Inspector. Well enough now. My associate and I are here to observe and offer our expertise when needed."

Swanson glanced at Ms. Rielly. "I see. Your associate?"

Ainsley gave her a sharp look and she jumped into speaking. "Dr. Rielly. Pleased to meet you, Chief Inspector. Feel free to, ahem, notify us should the need arise, yes?"

"A doctor? Huh. Our blasted physician cannot make it 'til the morrow. And it looks like another victim of the Torso Killer, too." Swanson cracked a toothy grin at the woman, eyeing her suspiciously. "Let us gain you entry, hm?"

Necessity did not take long to call and the two followed Swanson past the clout and into the less guarded construction zone. The ground was torn open with brick and mortar strewn about. The area had been cleared from the building they were renovating and their small group was quickly underground, into the older passages. The path was lit with lanterns and Swanson spent the journey explaining the events of the day.

The body had been discovered by a worker searching for his tools in the vaults early Monday morning. He had noticed a peculiar parcel deep in the vault multiple times on previous days but testified that he thought it a forgotten coat by another work fellow. On confirming it was not the other man's coat, they had come to inspect much to their surprise some contents of shocking value within the string tied wrappings.

"Like a sick gift," Swanson grimaced. "Hope you're none too delicate, *Doctor*."

Ms. Rielly stumbled a little over uneven stone. "I assure you, Chief Inspector, my own wrappings likewise conceal gristly contents."

They came to an erosion with wooden planks creating a bridge over it. On the other side, a thick vault waited quietly. Here, several lamps had been made available to shed clarity on the room.

The inspector cleared the bridge first. "In here is where she was found. Watch your step."

Ms. Rielly crossed precariously, with Lord Ainsley close behind. "*Her?*"

By the side of the vault, a large lump dressed in a dark rouge velvet lay still, straw strings tossed away. Ms. Rielly stopped short just a foot, a creeping cold nagging at the base of her instincts. She knew she was about to see a truly murdered body for the first time, one that could very well be the decaying remains of her friend. She took a breath and extended her hand, fingers shaking.

"I have seen all I need to, Chief Inspector," Lord Ainsley said.

Ms. Rielly jerked back, her fingertips just brushing the fabric. "What?"

Swanson echoed her sentiment. "You're finished? You haven't examined the body yet!"

"I am not here to examine your victim, Chief Inspector. That is not the job my credentials entail." He placed a hand on Ms. Rielly's shoulder and began leading her out. "Let me assure you, though, I have seen all I need to. And thus, Her Majesty has as well. I am sure I am correct in passing on her highest regards for the work you have done."

Swanson saluted. "Yes, sir, of course. We are ever grateful for Her Majesty's watchful eye."

With that, they were off the grounds and sliding into a dark buggy with Reginald at the reins.

"What do you mean you've seen all you needed to?" Ms. Rielly was about to burst. "You didn't even touch it!"

"We were not there to poke and prod the dear girl," Ainsley rubbed his eyes. "We were there for the scene, the modus operandi and the similarities we could trace between your friend's disappearance and this one. I did not have to touch her to deduce what we came for."

She could feel herself shaking, but from what she could not discern. "Then, may I ask, what has your deduction yielded?"

He sighed. "Starting with the wrappings: tailored burgundy velvet likely to originate in Kensington; heavy perfume not yet overcome by the damp, thus a recent kill. The perfume: a favorite, purchased in France. King's Honeywater, not a perfume commonly enjoyed by the masses. Which brings me to the important note: the woman's stature. Well-fed based on torso size and thus obviously belonging to a noblewoman. Your friend's killer has either changed in tastes or in identity altogether."

"There are two killers? Did we get this wrong?"

"Very likely, Ms. Rielly. However, I believe we have stumbled on to something very much to do with us." He bowed to hold his head in his hands. "Or, at least, myself."

Ms. Rielly stopped shaking with alarming clarity. "You… knew her? That's why you didn't need to look. That's how you knew so many details. You recognized her immediately!"

"Put your scalpel away, Ms. Rielly. I did not kill her."

She only then realized she had grabbed the tool from its concealment and blushed with embarrassment. "But how? This must be more than coincidence. You always seem to be the common denominator! Women disappearing into your home and now someone connected to you!"

Ainsley looked up and she stopped, shocked into silence by the depth of grief within his black eyes. "You do not yet have the full equation."

She gazed at him for understanding. "Then, please, Lord Ainsley. Tell me."

'Lord Ainsley and I returned to the Manor in quiet. His grief weighed down his face and yet I still knew not who he grieved for. But that grief was all too familiar, welling up inside his soul. How can I ever doubt him now? How can I point my finger at one who suffers so deeply? Was it possible the depth of despair emanating from his very soul was a mere pretense?

'No, even as my mind beats wildly against the truth, I know in my heart he is innocent of anything I might have thought him guilty of. Yes, he is hiding things. But has he murdered? No.

'Now what am I to do? On our journey to uncover Moira, it seems we have stumbled onto something even worse. Moira may be the victim of a prostitute killer, and a woman may have disappeared at one point into the Ainsley Manor, but who was this new woman? Why does this death change everything?'

***

"All right now, Jane. Open your eyes," Benjamin swept his hand from her face and she blinked them into focus.

Light dawned forth, illuminating the space before her. She laughed, taking it all in with joy. Moving mechanisms danced, dolls smiled at her, creatures of lore reached out to her. Paintings and backdrops, carpentry and props, whistles and noise makers. She touched each one and ran to return to him.

"He said yes!"

Benjamin grinned. "John said yes. He's behind this all the way. He said he wants to help me discover more about moving pictures and how they work. He sent this all from America!"

"Oh, Ben!" She took his hands and danced with him. "Your brilliant mind will provide the stories! Make your dreams reality! And then you could give others their dreams too!"

He laughed and picked her up, swinging her until they collapsed. They stared at each other and at the room. Benjamin watched her, his eyes wide as if trying to memorize her every detail. Her skin, the color of her eyes, the way her upper lip disappeared when she smiled.

"There is only one more dream I have," he spoke, sitting them up and taking her hand. "And it is a dream I hope to share with but one person."

Jane's face slowly reddened. "You cannot mean…"

"I have asked your mother and now I ask you: Jane Alice Peighton, will you live out our dreams with me forever?"

**

Lord Ainsley could still feel her sweet kiss. He stood at a mirror in his quarters, glaring at the man he saw. Where was the truth inside the blackness? Would he never be able to escape? Would everyone around him suffer the same fate?

He placed a hand on the cool glass and pressed, exerting a strength known only to him. The glass cracked and gave way and he let a piece take a nip of his finger. The blood came as it always did, quick and black. Ainsley watched as the wound bled, his heart pounding and breath coming fast. He glanced up to his reflection once more and accepted what was there: a different man than he used to be.

Chapter Six
Friend of My Enemy

Ms. Rielly awoke to Reginald standing over her with a tray of tea. She jolted up, pulling the blankets around her. "Reginald! I could have struck you!"

"Fear not, miss, for you did not." He offered the tea. "Lord Ainsley wishes to see you as soon as you are decent."

"He does?" She leapt from the bed, throwing on a robe. "Boggers being decent! I've waited long enough!" She rushed from the room. "Apologies, Reginald!"

"Not to worry, miss," he said to the empty room. "I shall follow at my own pace."

Ms. Rielly found Lord Ainsley in his study, perusing maps and faded letters. "Good morning! What is it? Are you well?"

He chuckled. "I had hoped the tea would delay you a spell. I should not have been surprised. At your promptness nor your robe."

She cleared her throat, tightening the robe self-consciously. "Yes, well. You are not often surprised." She calmed herself and took a seat. "Please do not beat about the bush this time, Lord Ainsley. I'm likely to go crazy what with."

"I will answer you," Ainsley said. He gathered the maps, sliding them into a drawer, and leaned against the bookshelf. "The woman who fell prey to our new predator was an old friend of mine. I am certain by this time you may assume I knew the killer. I do not."

"How could you not? The killer would have to know you personally to target someone you knew so well!" Ms. Rielly was quieted by Reginald's hand on her shoulder.

Ainsley continued. "I cannot draw conclusions as of yet. If I were to go by your hypothesis, we would be sifting through a great list of people for much time. I am certain, however, that our victims have different killers."

Ms. Rielly waited to speak. "Who was she? What was her name?"

Lord Ainsley turned away. "I will remind you of this only once, Ms. Jekyllyne Rielly. Do not question me... please."

Reginald said softly, "We do not speak of the dead here, Miss. My lord will answer everything in due time. He only tells you what you must know."

"Our next move," Ainsley pushed an envelope across his desk toward her.

She opened the ornate seal and read the contents. "We are to go to a ball?"

"I have rekindled some old connections that shall be attending. I believe we shall be able to find out more about both of our killers this way." He paused. "Honestly, Ms. Rielly, if the latest victim was targeted because of me, I would like to find out why."

"So we go to a ball," Ms. Rielly sighed. "I am going to need a new dress."

The Almack's Assembly Rooms gathered society's finest every Wednesday. The dancing was unexcitable and the dining sparse, but the entry alone was the item on everyone's agenda. Being seen with an admittance voucher from the Lady Patronesses of Almack's was akin to gaining the approval of the Queen herself.

Ms. Rielly fidgeted with her petticoats, searching the woman in the mirror for some pity. "He said he'd take care of the dress, didn't he? I should be grateful my purse remains intact. But what does he know of chenille stitches, satin pleats, and panniers? We may be going to the dullest and monotonous club in all of England, but it is still Almack's! What does he expect me to wear? How did he even gain entry in the first place?"

A soft knock came at the door and Reginald entered bearing a large box. "As we are short staffed with women, I behest your patience and assure you of my practice in such adornments."

Ms. Rielly laughed in nervous relief. "I was wondering who would tighten my corset! I trust you, my dear Reginald, but let us see what the lord has chosen for me."

She lifted the top to release the layers of fabric within. She reached slowly to press the silks between her hands, struck with awe. A rich caramel and gold *robe a la francaise* lay at her fingertips, ornamental floral patterns rushing over each fold, intricate yet simple. A tight bodice accompanied the beautiful dress and its ribboned petticoat.

"You'll have to abandon your current underdress for this one," Reginald said. "Alas, you might commit a fashion faux pas, yes?"

Ms. Rielly found her voice. "Wh-where did he find such a wonderful dress?"

"My dear," Reginald smiled. "My lord does not find such a thing. For a lady like yourself, he has it made."

The evening was just beginning to stretch its warming muscles when an extravagant carriage drawn with a four-horse team departed Ainsley Manor. For this occasion, a hansom cab and driver were hired to bring them to their destination. Reginald was to accompany Lord Ainsley inside the event and discreetly await any moment the lord might need him. The hansom was hired through the entirety of the evening and would wait nearby to escort them home when all was concluded.

Ms. Rielly tried desperately not to stare at Ainsley as he sat across from her. To say nothing of the evening before them and its impending surprises, she was once again captured by the sheer stature of the man. He had met her at the manor door in the most flattering attire, all dark hues of course, and she had been undone ever since. Even then, sitting across the way, she couldn't help but marvel at his confident posture and the unending feeling of possibility surrounding him.

She averted her gaze only to rest it on his hands. Hands that had once gripped a ship's railing, once shot game on a safari, once grasped at the world and all it had to offer. Hands that had held her scalpels, caught her waist as she'd fallen, and now helped her to dig for the truth.

Perhaps she would never stop wondering who the man really was. Perhaps he would forever be some truth she only half understood. But then, perhaps she did not fully know herself either, so how could she expect to truly know another?

Yet, as the carriage pulled alongside the steps of Almack's, she glanced at her reflection in the little glass window and knew one thing: that whoever she was to be, that night she could do anything. Because that night, as Ainsley met her by the manor door, he had called her beautiful.

Almack's atmosphere was bright and bold. The usual understated decor had been replaced by more titillating dressings. The food, too, had been upgraded from bread and cheese to cutlets and wine. Everyone there expressed their delight at the sudden change. They knew such a display could only mean that all the Lady Patronesses would be in attendance. And that would mean an even greater guest would be among them as well.

Reginald distracted the man announcing the guests long enough for Lord Ainsley to sweep Ms. Rielly past. "We don't wish to draw unwanted attention to ourselves," he explained with a small smile.

He tucked an arm under hers, letting her hand rest on the back of his own. Ms. Rielly's dress floated over the tile. A string quartet was setting up in the Regency Room while the card tables were already attracting society's finest gamblers in the Blue Damask Room. The other rooms were likewise becoming quite busy, voices overlapping and toes touching. Laughter and gossip expanded across the walls and ceilings. The music began and there was little space for dancing, but that did not deter some.

"What a tizzy!" Ms. Rielly said excitably. "How have I arrived here?"

Lord Ainsley kept smiling but warned, "Head high, Ms. Rielly. Society does not blink."

She straightened. "Right, then. Who is it we are looking for?"

As she spoke, a thin man in a stiff brocaded jacket with a winged vest approached them. "I say, if the world does not end this very evening then the person before me is not Lord Benjamin Ainsley! How long has it been, dear man?"

"Too long, Baron Crensworth. May I introduce Ms. Rielly?" She curtsied as he went on. "It has been some time for us both, has it not?"

"The people have missed you," Crensworth smiled conspiratorially. "You must know your presence here has caused a stir. How did you ever procure admission? Does one of our great Lady Patronesses owe you a favor?"

Lord Ainsley let the insult fall, but not without his own backbiting reply. "Ah, Baron Crensworth, you have not changed. Surely this is a delightful reminder of just how generous the ladies are to allow ones such as us to return. After your gambling incident, people were sure the doors were closed to you forever. So nice to see you still have connections." He excused himself and swept Ms. Rielly to another corner.

"Goodness. My scalpel couldn't cut the tension between you two!" she whispered. "He is certainly not the one we await."

"Certainly not," Ainsley agreed. "My dear, while we are engaged this evening, you must realize who you accompany. I do not always meet with the highest of society's moralities. Just remember: when I tap your hand, you may curtsy. If I do not, you may practice quadrille on

66

their mother's graves for all the power they have over you. Here, you are royalty."

Her eyes widened. "Truly? Here I thought only the elite could gain a place in Almack's."

"In this room, some species of rat are more cordial. And certainly more preferable," he sighed. "I despise society."

"Is that not the whole truth behind Lord Ainsley in three words?" a voice caused them to turn to seek its origin. A young man stood appraising them, his accent American and impeccable, as were his features. "Benjamin. It is good to see you."

Ainsley stood there for a heartbeat as if he'd been shot. When he spoke, it was sudden and quiet. "Ms. Rielly, this is my longtime friend, Michael Peighton."

He discreetly tapped her hand and she curtsied hastily. "Pleased to make your acquaintance, ahem, sir?"

The man smiled, shockingly handsome and friendly. He took her hand to kiss it. "Good guess, Lady Rielly. I am entitled 'Sir.' Where are Benjamin's manners?"

Lord Ainsley cleared his throat. "My apologies, Sir Peighton. I heard only recently of your knighthood by Her Grace."

"Please, Benjamin, to you I am always Michael. Her Majesty cannot change that." He laughed. "I myself still find getting settled into Her Highness' Special Armed Forces quite the queer routine."

"My, what an honor!" Ms. Rielly said. "Yet, you wear not the uniform?"

"You have a quick one on your arm, Benjamin," Michael jested. "No, Lady Rielly, I am of a small divisional force really. A plain coat, you might say. Here, you see?" He flashed a small badge pinned to the interior of his coat.

Ms. Rielly lit up but chastised him lightly. "Sir Peighton must know now I am no Lady of the Court. I am merely Ms. Rielly."

"Not so," he disagreed. "Any woman whom Lord Ainsley makes welcome is surely a lady to me."

He bowed and Ms. Rielly blushed. "I know not what to say!"

"Say you'll join me for a dance."

She blustered a little, looking to Ainsley who nodded and informed her, "The next song shall be a waltz."

Ms. Rielly thanked her stars internally, for the waltz was the only dance she surpassed in, and accepted Michael's offer. Lord Ainsley smiled as the two disappeared, but the mask fell away as they receded into the crowd and his thoughts swallowed him in its stead. Years had passed since he'd last seen Michael Peighton. A poisonous ache filled his chest upon remembering their final parting.

Ainsley broke away from his suffering when Reginald came to his side. "My lord, our friend has arrived. He awaits you in the gambling room. Shall I fetch your purse strings?"

"Not this night, Reginald. I came not to gamble with him, thank you." He crossed the room carefully and entered the games room.

This room was louder and more boisterous, with the added component of strong spirits. Some men smoked and some just chewed the ends of unlit cigars, betting on the cards. The room was hard to maneuver through, but Ainsley located the man he was meeting quickly.

They clapped hands together in a fierce handshake and Ainsley greeted him. "Alan!"

"Ben!" Alan had grown older in the separation of time, but he still kept a mischievous glint in his eye. "Where on earth have you been? I barely recognized you!"

"I am sorry it has been so long," Ainsley said, smiling genuinely.

"It matters not! I've been out of country with affairs of business for some time now anyway." He gasped, "Oh, but I've returned with Michael! We ran into one another amid my last trip and we've been back not a fortnight. He was off in the war, doing all sorts of thing for the queen, you know!"

"Yes, I'd heard he had returned to be knighted. It is fortunate you have come back as well," Ainsley said.

"Oh, yes. The war and all. I've done my bit and earned my business. No thanks to Her Royal Highness." He laughed. "It is good to be back and doing work in London again. And to be in good company! Michael is such a dull fellow to have as a bunk chap on the boat. Hard to believe a Yank is working for the queen, but such is how things are going nowadays. I suppose it helps to have family history in our fair England."

"I'm sure he's been working toward this day for a long time." Ainsley placed a hand on Alan's shoulder. "I am glad to see you, friend. I hope you'll forgive me for steering this conversation toward business."

Alan winked. "Business is what I excel at. Let us find a quiet place."

By this time, Ms. Rielly and Sir Peighton were enjoying the finishing strokes of their waltz. The music ended and the dancers clapped, dispersing or readying for the next set.

Michael pulled Ms. Rielly away, grabbing them both glasses of wine. She thanked him but only twirled the crystal in her fingers.

"Thank you for such a lovely waltz, Lady Rielly. You are truly talented." Michael sipped the red liquid. "I am curious to know how long you have known Benjamin."

"I am interested to know that of you, as well," she replied coolly. "You are an old friend?"

"Yes. Benjamin has known me since my youth. Long before I decided to make England my home," he said. "But that is history. What has Benjamin been preoccupying himself with these days? Did he ever take that journey to the islands of the aborigine?"

"I'm afraid he's been to such a lot of places; I can hardly keep track!" She let the feel of her hidden scalpel calm her. She couldn't very well let on that they were investigating murder. "And may I ask, what brought you to finally take England as your home?"

Michael's smile was devastating. "My late sister loved this country. She said the rain only served to let it grow on you."

"What a lovely saying. Sounds like London," she agreed. "Moss on every surface!"

He chuckled with her. "You may have heard Benjamin mention her in passing. Her name was Jane Peighton."

"Oi, there! Michael!" Alan called over as he and Ainsley joined them. "Who is this flower? Where did you find this one, Ben?"

Ms. Rielly raised an eyebrow. "*Ben?*"

Ainsley spoke over his friend. "Ms. Rielly, this is an old business partner, Alan Foster. Please excuse his candor."

Alan kissed her hand slowly. "*Je suis etoudi par votre beaute.*"

She looked puzzled. "That sounded like a compliment. Should I slap him, Lord Ainsley?"

"Worry not," Michael spoke up. "Your honor remains intact. He simply said, 'I am dumbfounded by your beauty.'"

She blushed at Michael.

"How is it I said the words, and yet this man here gets the credit?" Alan laughed. "My boy, Michael. Have you already made plans for which companies you'll be utilizing while you're in London?" He rounded an arm over Michael's neck, leading him off. "I'll be sure to find you later, Ben."

Ms. Rielly rubbed the hand he'd kissed on her skirts. "He's rather loud."

Ainsley nodded. "Reminds me of someone I know. Are you drinking?" He motioned at the wine.

She scoffed. "Of course not! Never drink when knowledge must be acquired." She gave it to him. "That Alan fellow is the one you mentioned? The one we are meeting?"

"Yes, Alan is a man of many talents, one of which is information." Lord Ainsley set the glass on a table. "I've already gleaned much. We aim to meet later in a more private setting."

"Why couldn't we have met him elsewhere in the first place? Sir Peighton was asking me many questions." She spoke hurriedly. "He wasn't alarming in any way. He is a delightful, well-versed man. I was only afraid to cause some unknown misstep of conversation."

Ainsley looked over the party with no answer.

Ms. Rielly's wit soon provided another realization. "You came because of him. You knew Sir Peighton would be here tonight. Is it true you have known him since he was a child?"

"I've had dealings with the Peighton family and sub-family in many forms in the past," Ainsley admitted. "Alan, himself, is Michael's cousin."

"I see." She gazed at the crowd then addressed him again. "Then, you must have known Sir Peighton's late sister, Jane."

Ainsley's eyes widened. "He spoke of her?"

"Just that she'd been to England before and that she was the deciding factor in his coming here." She searched his face. "Are you all right? Did you know her well?"

Lord Ainsley took up the wine glass and drank. "No matter now. I'll finish the meeting with Alan and arrange the carriage to take you home accompanied by Reginald to see to your safe return."

"What? I'm not privy to this meeting anymore?" She crossed her arms. "Then what was I here for? So you might have a pretty 'flower' on your arm?"

"I won't have you accost me here." He raised a hand to an unseen Reginald. "It is done. You will go now."

Reginald appeared at her elbow. "I shall take you home, Miss."

Her anger written all over her face, she followed the butler out, a storm brewing inside her. Her heels clicked sharply on the wet cobblestone as she fumed to the carriage. Torn between his assignment and remaining at the beck and call of his dear master, he elected to confirm the address with the hansom driver and watch as he departed with his feminine fare down the street. Only once the carriage had disappeared into the foggy evening did he turn his sights back to the estate and reenter. And only then did Ms. Rielly halt the carriage and exit.

Inside Almack's, Lord Ainsley once again commandeered a bit of space with Alan Foster.

"You sent the girl home?" Alan asked. "I thought she was involved in this."

"The night has become more complicated than I'd first calculated. It's better this way," Ainsley said. "Now tell me again."

"The lady of the night Ms. Rielly was acquainted with chose the wrong profession," he began. "London is not safe if you are of the moonlit rendezvous. Some of the badged men I know seem to think she fits the description of a certain Ripper victim."

"So, it's true?"

Alan nodded. "Her identity was difficult to discover, but my sources are certain. And unless you're going to track down the Ripper himself, or herself, your line on this one has been cut. Depends on how much Ms. Rielly was expecting from this and how far she expected to go."

"I have a feeling she might have come to the same conclusion soon. Her friend's death may have been what brought her here, but now she stays for something deeper. Hopefully, the knowledge alone of her friend's fate will suffice. The Ripper is out of our reach. We cannot hunt down some creature a sane person will never understand," he reasoned. "Now, what of the other?"

"Yes. My sources say there is also another ripper of sorts. They're calling him the Torso Killer. You've heard of him I see. But, given the victim and the timing, this one seems too suspicious."

"Timing?"

Alan came closer, speaking in an undertone, his expression grave. "Something is happening, Ben. I have connections everywhere and you know my business doesn't discriminate across the line of the law. The people I've been in contact with are not happy, on either side. I cannot be sure, but it all seemed to coincide with Sir Michael's return."

"What does the killing have to do with Michael? He's only just returned to England," Ainsley said.

"Do you understand the special force he has been appointed to head, Ben? Do you know what it's for? Or how he even got the job?" He leaned in.

Lord Ainsley clenched his teeth behind pursed lips. "I can only guess."

"Listen to me, Ben," said Alan. "The killing itself was obviously not perpetrated by him, but things could get very dangerous for us both should we pry more. It is too soon to tell anything definite."

"I have to know why she was killed, Alan. What could she possibly have been involved in that led to her murder?" he wondered aloud. "What other connection to danger is there, other than that she was my acquaintance?"

"It is like I said, Ben, both sides of the law are being disturbed. It is most likely she was killed by the darker side." He explained, "My sources say a group of certain powerful means has begun to move since Michael's return.

These men do not have codes of ethics. Michael may have had dealings with your victim and they used that to extrapolate findings of their own." He paused, putting a comforting hand on Ainsley's arm. "You know she was a wily old bat. She knew the Peightons better than anyone and longer than you. I'm sorry about what happened to her, Ben."

Ainsley only nodded, unable to respond.

"In all likelihood, Ben, it was her ties to Michael that led to her murder."

"If only I knew what Michael is getting into or even what this group has to do with all of this. You said you're still working on getting information?" Ainsley prompted, to which Alan nodded.

"Let me just say one last thing I think you should be aware of, Ben. I don't know if it matters to you, but Michael kept asking me about a specific trip that I wasn't aware you had taken. He said you had supposedly soloed it. I told him I had no idea, or course. Do you know of what he speaks?"

"No," Ainsley said. "I can't recall."

"Well, I suppose that is for the best. If my information is correct, this mystery may start making sense very soon. I have people investigating exactly what Michael is involved in and that underground group." He sighed. "Unfortunately, some of my sources are slower than others. Getting information on Michael is almost as hard as getting the jewels from the queen."

"What about me now?" Michael walked to them through the thinning crowd.

Ainsley straightened unconsciously. "I hope Ms. Rielly treated you well."

"Very. She is a wonderful dancer." He smiled. "You two must be catching up. I haven't interrupted, have I?"

"Of course not!" Alan blustered. "This man here does nothing excitable anymore. It's like he has grown old in my absence!"

"Yes, I was regaled on the entirety of your adventures together on the way here," Michael said. "Not to change a very well-known subject, but I have not seen Lady Rielly since the dance. I had thought she'd be with you, Benjamin."

Ainsley answered his implied question, "Yes, Ms. Rielly had to call an early night. My butler escorted her home."

"Are you certain?" Michael asked. "Because I see your manservant just over there when a carriage ride should have delayed him longer."

Ainsley caught a glimpse of Reginald across the rooms through an arched doorway and his heart nearly froze. He didn't want to reveal the panic he felt, but still chose to excuse himself quickly. He did so with an apology and came to the butler with but one concern, which he voiced.

"Where is she?"

"I sent her home, my lord. Quite some time ago," he responded. "You are distressed?"

"Yes, and rightly so." He almost paced. "Do you not remember the woman we are dealing with, Reginald? I should not have sent her away in the first place. This is my fault alone."

"What would you like to do, sir?"

Ainsley thought for a moment. "Find the cabbie and ascertain if she disembarked. Question everyone with her description. If she is not here…" He banished the thought. "I shall go back to Alan and apprise him of the situation. Then we shall spread out to find her. Now, go!"

He immediately went back to where Alan and Michael still conversed. Alan lit up. "Good, you've returned. Locate our dear flower?"

"Yes, all is well. I leave for the manor myself." He motioned. "Join me for a moment, Alan?"

As they walked away, Ainsley filled him in. "She's disappeared? With a killer stalking the streets of London?"

"I have Reginald checking she is truly gone, but it appears she did not return to Almack's," Ainsley said. "If you cannot get away, I shall search myself. Please use all the tools you have at your disposal. You understand the gravity of this."

Alan guffawed. "Of course I can get away. If Michael were a dog upon my ankle, I'd chop off the limb! Leave it to me, Ben."

Reginald came to his side just as Alan left it. "The carriage let her off almost a block away, sir. Shall I pursue her most likely course?"

"Alan is going to tap his network for any sightings and I shall search for her. Please go back to the manor in case she returns. Find us again should she be there."

Reginald departed with a nod. Alan and Ainsley left Almack's just after the clocks of their dark world struck ten. The hunt was on.

Chapter Seven

'It Is Love That I Am Seeking for, but of a Beautiful, Unheard of Kind.'

William Butler Yeats

Jekyllyne let her fingers caress the leaves and flowers as she passed them. Moonlight served as her only guide, but she cared not where she went. The night sounds carried her away on the notes of their symphony. She twirled, the skirt of her dress expanding. Her shoes were muddy and her pleats torn as if she had fallen several times. Her eyes were glossy and cheeks red, her breath leaving wisps of white vapor as she moved.

She stumbled and a hand caught hers. She smiled and melted into the arms, whispering happily, "Benjamin!"

He took her waist and they began to dance, spinning together around the flowers. She giggled gaily as they spun, faster and faster. Then he was letting her go and her hands searched frantically for his, her eyes wide as she fell.

She backed into a solid body and arms closed around her once again. She turned to laugh at how he had frightened her when the face she saw twisted unnaturally. She screamed, the arms tightening around her until she couldn't breathe. The face smiled menacingly, its teeth razor sharp.

"Ms. Rielly!" it roared.

She fought its deadly grasp. "No! Don't kill me!"

"Ms. Rielly! It is I!" it yelled again, shaking her. "Ainsley!"

Ms. Rielly ceased her fighting, blinking at him through the haze. "It is you, Benjamin! You gave me such a fright!" She threw her arms around him. "Please don't do that again!"

Ainsley gasped despite himself. He wasn't sure whether he was shocked by her pronouncing his name for the first time or by her sudden embrace. He pushed her away gently, holding her at arm's length and examining her eyes. "Have you been drugged?"

She smiled at him, swaying a little. "Shall we continue our dance, Benjamin? You dance quite well for such a stiff."

He wrapped her in his coat and picked her up. "Come, Ms. Rielly. We shall continue our dance at home."

She laughed, blushing. "Oh, Benjamin, call me Jekyllyne!"

Ainsley held her close and left the park he'd found her in. He hailed a hansom and slid carefully inside. By the time they had reached the manor, Ms. Rielly had fallen asleep with her head resting on his lap.

Ms. Rielly pushed through the thickest veil of sleep she'd ever known the next morning. She ached all over and noticed vaguely that she'd been changed into nightwear. She stood, wobbling on her complaining feet. Her knees were bruised and she plucked a twig from her hair.

In that moment, she realized she was not alone. She turned to see Ainsley sleeping in the chaise by her hearth, breathing softly. She had never before seen him so vulnerable. She gazed at him, tip-toeing closer, but her feet were as heavy as lead and she tripped.

Ainsley's eyes unclosed. "Ms. Rielly?" He stood up quickly and went to her side. "Are you all right? How are you feeling?"

She chuckled nervously. "I'm not quite sure how to answer that. Perhaps you can tell me what happened last night?"

He sat her down on the chaise. "You remember nothing?"

She touched her forehead. "I... can't recall... I'm not sure."

He nodded. "That is all right. I can fill in some of the missing details and see if anything comes to light." She nodded back at him in approval. "Do you remember leaving the party?"

"Yes," she groaned. "You made me leave! Why did you do such a thing! I have just as much invested in this as you!"

"That doesn't matter for now. Please, Ms. Rielly, tell me: do you remember Kensington Gardens?" He kneeled in front of her.

"Kensington?" Her eyes widened. "Ainsley, what has happened to me? What does the garden have to do with this?"

"It's all right," he said calmly. "You did not come to any harm, save for some scrapes from landscaping. It does appear, however, that you were drugged in some way."

"Drugged?" She jumped up but immediately fell back into the seat, dizzy.

Ainsley continued in the same comforting voice, "Just rest. When you left the party, did something happen?"

She clenched her eyes shut. "I don't understand any of this. Did you not see me? I followed you from Almack's."

Now he stood. "What?"

"I remember…" she spoke slowly, "I was so mad, you know! I was going to stomp right up to you and say so! But before I reached the doors, I saw you. You looked right at me, I swear. And then you began walking away so I followed you and called after you. Then…" she held her head. "Then you vanished… that can't be possible. And I was dancing… I think." A horrified look crossed her face. "Oh! There was a monster!"

Ainsley took her hands. "It's all right, Ms. Rielly. You don't have to try any longer. I believe that sometime between the carriage and the doors to Almack's, someone must have drugged you. You were hallucinating."

She searched his eyes, her own appearing lost. "It was like a dream and a nightmare all at once. I could have sworn it was real…"

"Do not worry. We shall find out what really happened," he reassured her. "We are just relieved you did not come to any worse harm."

"Why, the person who did this is fortunate!" she growled. "When I find them, I'll show them what a scientist can do!"

Ainsley smiled. "I am glad you seem unaltered. And we are not without theories as to why this came about."

"Yes?" She perked up.

"You remember Alan Foster from the party."

She nodded.

He continued, "Alan was helping to organize the search for you and we planned to meet back at the manor by midnight no matter the progress. Alan, however, has not shown. This can only lead me to think that the true target was Alan and you were a distraction."

"That makes sense, if the information he had was as valuable as you think," Ms. Rielly said.

Just then, the bell of the front door rang. A floor below them, Reginald answered. Voices were muffled and difficult to distinguish.

Ainsley headed for her door. "I shall go see who has come."

Ms. Rielly agreed. "I will join you once I have dressed."

Ainsley left the room, stopping briefly at the stairwell to listen and identify the voice. Once he achieved this, he steeled himself for the encounter ahead. He descended the stairs with a practiced smile.

"Michael. Good to see you."

Reginald introduced the guest, "Sir Peighton, milord. Shall I prepare the tea room?"

"Please," Ainsley beckoned. "While Reginald prepares, let us adjourn to the study."

Michael smiled. "I apologize for my unannounced visit."

They went to the study and sat across from each other. The air was charged with tension, but both men maintained friendly nonchalance. An imaginary chess game had begun.

"I hope Lady Rielly was located without much difficulty," Michael said. "I was stopping by to offer my assistance."

"A wonderful offer, really, but too late in its arrival. We found her well enough ourselves. Just a misunderstanding in truth. The hansom driver mistook the address so she had begun to walk but became turned about. I appreciate your concern for Ms. Rielly."

"Of course, Benjamin. I am happy she is well." He narrowed his eyes, still smiling. "Not to mention you."

"I am afraid I don't understand your meaning."

"When you had discovered her gone," Michael explained, "I had never seen you so distressed. I refer now to your more evened emotional state. You must be at ease to know she is safe."

"Yes," Ainsley said shortly. "I am much calmed by her safety."

The door opened and Ms. Rielly entered. "Not gossiping about me, are you?"

They both stood on ceremony and Michael stepped forward to greet her. "Lady Rielly. So good to see that last night's excitements did no harm. Benjamin has informed me of your confusing adventure."

"Has he?" She eyed the other man nervously.

"I hope you'll never again get so lost," Michael said. "Where did you say you found her, Benjamin?"

She laughed lightly. "Kensington, apparently."

"Apparently?" Michael raised an eyebrow. "You don't know?"

Ms. Rielly stammered. "I was so tired, you see. And it was so dark. I very nearly fainted."

Michael nodded slowly, as if trying to grasp the concept. At that point, Reginald came to announce the tea room was ready. The butler led the guest first, with the other two trailing behind to whisper.

"How long shall we be expecting to entertain our guest?"

Ainsley almost shrugged but held it back, not yet tired enough to forget his manners. "We must show him a well enough time, Ms. Rielly. You understand."

"Yes, well I also understand that yet another person who knows you has gone missing," she hissed. "We have work to do!"

They were nearing the room when the doorbell rang again and Reginald excused himself to answer it. He returned promptly and presented Ainsley with the post. The envelope was unmarked.

Ms. Rielly broke the silence, "Sir Peighton, will you be making London your permanent home even after the conclusion of your business here?"

Michael nodded. "Yes, but only because my business will not likely end until I retire." He checked his pocket watch. "Which reminds me: I cannot stay for tea. I must be going but first, Ms. Rielly," he took her hand, "I reiterate my utmost happiness that you are safe and sound." They saw him to the door and Michael thanked them. "Benjamin, now that I am local, I hope we shall be seeing more of each other."

The door had barely closed when Ms. Rielly pounced on the letter. "Who is it from?"

Lord Ainsley ignored the question and went back to the study, Ms. Rielly nipping at his heels. He expertly brandished a sharp letter opener and swiped at the seal. He unfolded the parchment and read aloud.

"'Ben, apologies for not keeping our schedule last night but something has come up. I do wish with all my heart that our lovely flower has not come to untimely misfortunes. Sorry for the discordant nature of this note. I shall explain everything soon. We MUST meet. I shall send for you forthwith. Alan F.'"

The writing was hurried and scratched into the paper with reckless abandon, broken through in some places. Ainsley offered it to Ms. Rielly. She read it through repeatedly to herself.

"Seems he was rushed," she said. "What shall we do? Just wait for his call?"

"I suppose that is all we should do," Ainsley replied. "Alan has yet to play his cards."

"Well, then," she pulled a needle from her sleeve, "will you help me draw some blood? If there are any traces of drugs remaining in my system, I am the person to find them!"

Ainsley took the needle and helped her tie a tourniquet she produced from yet another hidden place. "Will you be able to identify the differences?"

"I've studied my own blood many times," she said proudly. "I could identify one drop of my own among a bucket of a pig's!" The needle slipped under the skin and she gasped.

Ainsley halted. "Are you alright? Have I done it wrong?"

"No," she said in wonderment, "I remembered something. A needle... a pinch on my neck." The unseen memory flashed within her eyes. "I saw him. Before I followed the man I thought was you. I saw Michael. He was speaking to someone at the door of Almack's and he looked at me and smiled. That's... that is all, I'm afraid."

Ainsley puzzled. "Michael was the one who alerted us to your disappearance. But he claimed his last sighting of you was when you danced with him." He finished drawing the blood and released her arm.

Ms. Rielly sighed. "Perhaps I was just hallucinating him too! I don't know what to trust of my recollections. I was also so sure I had danced with you!" She gasped, catching her slip too late.

"Quite all right, Ms. Rielly. You may have mentioned something of a dance when I had found you." He tried not to smile.

"I was drugged!" she huffed in her defense. "I am not at fault for anything I may have said or did!"

"Not at all," he said. "Jekyllyne."

Her face flushed. "What?"

"Oh, perhaps I am only permitted to call you that whilst you are under the influence of apothecaries." He let the smile grow.

"Enough, you! Whatever happened to that stick you had lodged so far—" she sighed, exasperated. "I will not be drawn off track!"

"Off track? Have I derailed you in some way?" Ainsley asked innocently. "I'd take kindly to your not speaking of sticks, by the by."

She composed herself. "How on earth did you find me, anyway? The gardens are a ways from Almack's."

"Alan had many eyes looking for you. I suppose I was fortunate in my heading," Ainsley said.

She crossed her arms, changing the subject. "Lord Ainsley, it is time. Let me draw your blood as well. Come now, do you not trust me after all this?"

He turned away but consented. "Yes, you are correct. I shall allow you a vial to study," he addressed her seriously. "Please understand this is of the utmost privacy. Whatever you find…"

She nodded. "This is our burden alone."

***

'Hematology. The study of blood, bone, body. Ahh, to return once again to the passion of my heart! Veins and arteries, throbbing delivery systems, leading like roads to the source of the beating within our breast! Garish and beautiful, vivacious yet fragile, a drop replaced and a liter lost.

'My vial in stark contrast to his own. Such secrets and answers to be unlocked within that darkness. I have obtained the effect, but what of the cause? Shall I uncover it as I peer through the microscope? I only hope!

'Lord Ainsley has set up a makeshift laboratory within his theater. He has magically procured medical instruments of dubious origins, but who I am to murmur? This is a dream out of my deepest subconscious!

'The study of my own blood is of an inconclusive nature. I have isolated the unknowns but am at an impasse as I have nothing to compare the particular poison to. I

87

further my studies by attempting a recreation of the compound with a similar structure, but alas I am no chemist.

'Ainsley's blood is entirely unfamiliar. But I may yet wring truth from its complicated strands! Ainsley himself has returned to his usual unreadable character. He is as frustrating and intriguing as his blood and I shall not acquiesce!

'Once again, he has rebuilt his wall. Just as I seem to scale it, I realize there is another! I think back to the name that had disrupted his façade at the ball. Jane Peighton. Perhaps an impromptu visit of my own is due.

'Alan has not yet called on us for a week.'

"This room has been here since I was a child," Lord Ainsley had entered the theater. "I can remember playing in it as my father worked."

"So your father built this place?" She looked around with new understanding. "He must have been a very interesting man."

"I wish I could attest to that," Ainsley admitted. "I don't believe I ever truly met the man. He was such an unreachable being to me when I was young."

"Lord Ainsley, I think…" she began speaking faster as she gathered her papers. "I think there is something we should discuss."

He turned to her slowly, as if caught in a predator's sights. "What about?"

Ms. Rielly sighed. "What is all this really?" She motioned to the theatre around them. "Why have you collected such an odd assortment? For whom are all these obviously distracting pleasures?"

Ainsley smiled a little. "They were once just as you described them. Such distracting pleasures. They were... a dream. One I had when I was quite a bit younger than I am now. Let me ask you: for what do you think all these items would be put to use?"

She blinked. "Pictures. Like the theatre optique. Did you intend to make something similar?"

His smile grew wider. "Not similar. Better. I desired to make pictures unlike anything anyone had ever seen. Full length shows that depicted lands no one here could ever dream of. Lands I had been to. Lands I imagine are still out there, waiting."

His face dropped. His eyes grew far away, staring out across the lifeless sea that had grown within him, never to see the light again. "But it was not to be. Now here they rest, perhaps to be sold someday. Perhaps to be buried."

Ms. Rielly had been smiling with him up until that moment, energized by his sudden excitement. When he once again shut himself in, she too drew back. "Why? Has your dream changed?"

He puzzled. "No, it has not. But something happened that I could never undo. And now it is impossible for me to go back."

She swallowed. "What happened, Lord Ainsley?"

His black eyes met hers. "I woke up."

Sir Michael Peighton had acquired apartments in London since realizing his work would require time; it was here that Ms. Rielly arrived. The rooms were sparse but dignified, on the second floor and usually centering around a piece of artwork or tapestry. Each one seemed purposeful, but spoke of alien tastes that did not quite fit together.

Peighton answered the door himself and ushered her through to the drawing room. This one appeared much more inhabited, organized but full to the brim with books speaking of a much-learned man. A lovely dark oak tea table was cleared and a maid set a tray down before leaving the two.

Ms. Rielly sat across from her host and sipped demurely, complimenting the taste.

"Thank you for coming," Michael said. "I am only saddened that our Lord Ainsley could not make the trip. Is he so preoccupied?"

"I barely see him myself. This last week has been busy for us both, I suppose," Ms. Rielly smiled. "I do hope I can fill the absence dutifully."

"I am sure you will suffice," he smiled back. "I am glad we could afford a better opportunity to speak. No loud crowds."

"Or chances of getting lost," she joked. "I still have much confusion over that night. Perhaps I had too much wine. I was sure you had spotted me outside before I left but Lord Ainsley informs me otherwise."

"I assure you, had I seen you I would have not let you go." Michael's light blue eyes were playful. "Your affirmed safety did much to settle my worries."

"Thank you, Sir Peighton. Again, you flatter me with such ease." She tried not to blush. "I am glad you did not think my informal visit improper."

"Please call me Michael. Sir Peighton seems too official. And if you think it not improper, may I call you Jekyllyne from now on?"

"I do admit conversation seems more comfortable that way," she responded. "Jekyllyne is better than Ms. Rielly."

"Very good." He sat back with a sigh. "This weather makes me very anxious. I am fortunate to have your calming presence."

Ms. Rielly put down her cup. "I am surprised you have such leisurely days to enjoy. Have you not been busy serving queen and country?"

"Yes, one would think Her Majesty keeps all her loyal subjects busy. However, my personal requirements allow me a day to myself once in a while. Although, the inactivity drives me mad."

"So you'd prefer to be at constant attention? Never a moment's rest?"

"Yes, I am guilty. I am not one to settle down and enjoy a simple life. I must always be chasing." He adjusted his posture. "And you? Does such inconsistency and instability not appeal?"

Ms. Rielly thought on herself. "Inconsistency is just another word for excitement in my dictionary. And as for instability, if one cannot adapt to the ever-changing world in which we live, then that person is a bore." She paused and he waited for her to elaborate. "I myself find that an uneven world makes for the most wonderful exertions of life-affirming action."

Michael smiled wide. "You are a most captivating young woman, Jekyllyne. Perhaps that is what draws him to you so."

Ms. Rielly's cheeks grew hot and she had a flash of paranoia toward the tea. She recovered and fixed her skirts, her fingers brushing the hidden scalpel. "And you, Sir Peighton? What draws you to Lord Ainsley?"

"I've made you uncomfortable," he acknowledged. "I apologize."

"Then atone for it," she suggested. "Tell me of your sister, Michael."

He sat staring at her for a moment and she almost began to regret the inquiry, but then he spoke, "I first met Benjamin when he came to visit our family in America. He was already close with my sister. She had begun staying in London with our mother more than at home. I always favored the states more, being born there. I was young and remember little, but I remember realizing how important he was to my sister."

Ms. Rielly sensed him becoming agitated. "I apologize. You don't have to tell me if it is too painful to speak of her."

Michael smiled sadly. "I have not had anyone to discuss this with in years. In truth, I miss it. I miss remembering her."

She swallowed hard. "How did she… pass?"

"She fell," he said simply. "Broken neck. No great mystery. Just gravity."

"I am sorry," she said again.

"The way I heard it she passed quickly. No pain," he said, his eyes unreadable.

"The way you heard it?"

"They had gone out of the country. To islands unknown to me. Father and I were only present when her body was returned to us. Mother had apparently known for a while, but the post does not travel quickly on ships," he explained.

"Benjamin... did not send word to describe in detail how it happened."

"Lord Ainsley?" Her heart skipped.

"Yes. She had gone on the trip with him, after all."

Silence grew between them. Michael looked at the floor. Ms. Rielly could not help but recognize the expression of grief.

"Do not trouble yourself, Jekyllyne," he said. "That was too long ago. Let us enjoy our tea."

"Yes, we should speak of lighter things on such a day, Michael." The name was sounding more natural as it rolled off her tongue.

He responded with a beaming grin, "The balance is restored. 'Let there be light!'"

Ms. Rielly giggled. "I suppose I owe you a bit for putting you through that. Ask me one question."

Michael became stone still. "Why are you really at Ainsley Manor?"

She smiled. "Silly, really. I am writing Lord Ainsley's memoirs. Although, it is proving difficult."

His demeanor transformed. Gone was the easy smile and relaxed posture. Before her now was the Queen's dog. "I mean your real reason. Benjamin may have had a most excitable life, but I highly doubt he could not find it in himself to pen them. I don't believe you realize just how dangerous it is for you to be near him, Jekyllyne."

Her hand quickly found the scalpel again and she looked away. "I only misunderstood your question. Please do not mistake my light words for a light mind."

"Please do not mistake my docility as being blind, Jekyllyne." He stood. "There is something not right with your presence in that place. I think only of your safety."

She too stood, now stronger in resolve. "Do not presume my safety is not already in capable hands. I believe my presence in that house is my own, Michael."

"I apologize, yet again. I am being too forward." He bowed. "I think it best your butler escort you home. Please take care."

His hard exterior had melted so easily back into the charming and sweet man that Ms. Rielly almost felt guilty. "My butler is not with me, so if you'd show me the door."

He acquiesced like a gentleman, leading her out before she stopped and placed a hand on his arm. "Please understand, Michael. There is much I may not know, but Ben is a good man."

He was smiling sadly again. "I do hope to see you again."

She nodded and left the apartments of Sir Michael Peighton.

***

"Ben!" Jane ran into his open arms. "This is so amazing! I've been so excited I could barely sleep! Tell me, where does this great swimming behemoth take us?"

Benjamin smiled. "Surely you'll deduce our destination once the captain has set a heading. You know, we shall be returning to a very incensed Madam Tusor."

"Oh, she knows very well if I am to become the next manager of Ainsley Manor I should start early! I need to learn what you do on these business trips!" She swatted away an imaginary vision of a steaming madam.

"And your mother was not all too grateful for this opportunity…"

"Ah, Mum," she scoffed. "She's just worried about her darling daughter's honor. I have you all to myself until the first stop and then her maid will be with us the rest of the way to interrupt. John and Michael don't even know, the post is so slow! Why bother sending letters when it is old news by the time it reaches them?"

"My dear Jane, I am not entirely sure what you think the maid shall be interrupting," his voice was cloying.

Jane leaned back into him, facing the wide sea. "Shall we shock them all? Shall we marry in some foreign land amid the wilds?" She sighed, speaking dreamily but with a hint of sadness.

The sound of the waves echoed in Lord Ainsley's ears as he sat, eyes closed, at his desk. Thoughts ran through him, wishes made long ago, like vicious burns, quick and freezing hot against his heart.

He knew they were on to something bigger. The answers lurked just beneath the surface, sneering and taunting them from unreachable lengths. For once in a long time, Ainsley felt the exhilaration that came alongside danger. He felt released from his previous ties, unsafe yet sure footed. This time, he swore he would not cause a death.

Chapter Eight

The Monster Orchestrates

"You have made a most correct choice in involving me fully this time. Really, it is just better for both of us," Ms. Rielly smiled, tucking freshly sharpened scalpels into the hidden pockets of her sleeves. "Although, I cannot claim I understand the thinking behind bringing Reginald. My apologies, Reginald, you know I have the utmost respect for you."

Reginald took no offense. "Yes, Ms. Rielly."

"Reginald has accompanied me on more than one of my more daring pursuits," Ainsley said. "He is, at times, like another appendage."

Ms. Rielly tugged at her cuffs. "Yes, well, at least you are sure of yourself. I must admit I am nervous. You said Alan had sounded normal?"

"He appeared undisturbed. Just pressed for time." Ainsley held out an umbrella. "I know it seems you've only just returned, but we must be going."

"I shall fetch a carriage," Reginald said, leaving quickly through the door so as not to allow the rain entry.

Ainsley turned to Ms. Rielly. "You vexed me greatly when I found you gone from the manor without so much as Reginald to escort you. Please repeat it."

She took a deep breath. "I shall stay with you or Reginald at all times. I shall never leave your sight. I will exercise care in all my actions. Is there anything I forgot, Lord Benjamin Ainsley III?"

When he placed his hands upon her shoulders, she snapped from snarky to serious, meeting his eyes. He stood so close she had to tilt her head up a little. She could smell the musk from his clothes and skin.

He spoke, "Promise me."

She nodded. "I promise."

She quietly added his name to her lips as he walked out, ensuring he did not hear.

Alan Foster straightened his vest, checking a pocket watch, trying to appear casual but secretly poised for action. He thought back to the old habit he used to have of chewing the end of a matchstick. Ainsley had always chastised him, warning him that one day he would set it alight and watch his mouth burn. He had eventually quit the habit only to replace it with a shilling that he twisted with his fingers.

The night's agenda was stretched before his mind's eye. He recited every detail over and over. They had to be cautious if what he knew was true. His delay had so far cost him, but he intended to make it up with careful planning.

He would meet with Ainsley alone in a small, little known park. Concurrently, Ms. Rielly and Reginald would await their return at The Lion's Boudoir, an upscale men's club that he frequented. They would be safest there while Alan shared his information, surrounded by many of his friends. If he had gone near the manor, all would have been lost. The noisy pitter patter of the rain would grant them some cover at least.

At the park, Alan would share all the information he had attained with Ainsley. There, he would show him the proof, the most vital piece and the reason why they met alone. All would go according to plan if he had been diligent.

Alan watched the foggy gray silhouettes of people passing from his chosen spot. No one looked his way, their minds preoccupied with their own daily doings. So close to the people who lived dangerously, yet unaffected by them. Blissfully unaware. He stood apart, but not too far from foot traffic. Even then he second-guessed his placement, worrying that he was not close enough to the periphery of the public eye. But it had to be here.

The city was held back only by the flimsy looking stakes of wrought-iron fences. Most were reclaimed by nature and tilting permanently amid the decomposition. The surrounding buildings were old brick tenements, mostly abandoned. No one would tear the remnants down. A perfect representation of Alan's own business: a decaying necessity surrounded by the forgotten.

His gaze took in a figure coming into focus and he felt himself physically relax when he recognized Ainsley. Their umbrellas met and the two exchanged formalities.

"Has our dear flower and her guard found the Lion well?"

"Yes, they have reached their destination in one piece." Ainsley internally cursed the wet spreading in his shoes.

"I hope the young lady doesn't find the accommodations too appalling," Alan chuckled nervously.

Ainsley sighed. "Honestly, she has been in worse environments. She shall be outwardly displeased, but inwardly sating an unquenchable curiosity."

Alan squared off with him to urgently attend to their business. "We need to converse quickly and reconvene with the other members of our party. They should be safe at the club at the moment, but if what I know is true, then we are all in peril. Contacts underground have begun to move, very specific ones. Someone has suddenly begun to pull strings long since left to rot. People are being silenced, Ben, and they all have one thing in common: the Ainsley name."

Ainsley was intent to learn more but still voiced a theory pressing insistently at the corners of his mind. "This all began when Michael came back. Do you think someone is targeting us because of him?"

Alan became frantic at this query, his tone turning curt. "No, no. Michael is all wrong! He does not realize who he is chasing! I've buried the truth where only you can find it. Focus on the name!" As he paused for breath, a shot rang out: unnatural and piercing.

Ainsley's mind calculated the only possible source for such a noise as Alan crumpled to the wet ground, a budding red flower cresting over his chest. Ainsley dropped to him, pressing into the wound as Alan paled. He searched fiercely for the origin of the gunshot.

Alan shuddered. "Ben, my brother. Look twice. Your father's…"

The words faded with Alan's soul. Whistles were sounding shrilly, but Ainsley paid no heed. Even as the copper clapped irons around his wrists, his eyes never left the man who had been his compatriot for so long. He glanced briefly at the gate across the way that read 'King's Cemetery,' where the Ainsley predecessors lay in rest.

"What are you doing in here, Benjamin?"

Young Ben startled, whirling to put his hands behind his back. "Nothing, Father."

The elder Ainsley smiled gently. "Come now. Show me what you've found." He knelt to come face to face with the boy.

Benjamin revealed the mouse inside his hands reluctantly. "I found her in your study, Father. I'm sorry I went in there."

"It's all right, my boy." He watched the small creature twist through Benjamin's fingers. "How do you think she got there?"

"From the basement," Benjamin answered quietly.

"Yes. From the basement where I work. And what does that mean?" he prompted.

"That she belongs to you."

"Very good." His father extended an open and waiting hand. "She's very important to my work, Benjamin. You wouldn't want my work to be affected, correct?"

"No." The boy let the mouse drop into the hand and smiled. "Will you let me come see?"

"Not today," the lord said, standing. "But soon. When the mice are gone you can come down again."

Benjamin heard the mouse squeak. "Where do they go?"

His father looked at him. "They go home."

"Mighty suspicious. A man of your status being called a murderer. Quite suspicious." Chief Inspector Swanson puzzled over the sight of Lord Ainsley in his jail.

"I assure you, Chief Inspector, this is all a case of a serious misunderstanding." He had been released from the irons, but now looked out from between bars. "Your fellow officer is just mistaken. I could not have committed this act."

"He's covered in the victim's blood, sir. And refuses to reveal his name!" The fellow officer in question defended from behind the chief, as if afraid to get near Ainsley. He was quite a sight to behold with his black stare whispering of death and similarly dark clothes.

"Balderdash, Pellier! Why, I've met the man just the other day. Isn't that correct, ahem, what was your name? Please forgive me, I only saw it once," the chief blundered a little.

"Highly suspicious, sir," Pellier inserted.

"Perhaps…" Swanson cleared his throat. "In any case, you shall have to consent to a finger printing."

"Visitor, sir!" Another watchman appeared at the door, sounding off. "A Ms. Rielly."

"Ah! Let her in." She came through and the chief addressed her directly. "Dr. Rielly. A name I do remember. You realize I mustn't allow you contact with the suspect. Perhaps you can shed some light on the situation here."

Ms. Rielly ignored his inquiry. "Indeed, I thank you for your graciousness in the request. I am here for evidence, of course. I must gather it as quickly as possible." She brandished a scalpel and kerchief. "To compare samples. May I?"

She didn't wait for the gruff sound of his decision to kneel immediately in front of Ainsley. She reached through the bars for the sleeve of his coat, cold with perspiration.

She sensed that Swanson's original suspicion for her doctorate may be resurfacing.

Ainsley whispered, barely audible as the other men in the room conversed with Swanson. "Dig up my father's grave. King's Cemetery. Do not go alone."

A commotion outside the holding area drew the chief away, but the hawk-nosed Pellier narrowed his eyes on them, not budging an inch.

"Almost done now," Ms. Rielly said. She cut a swatch of fabric to fold into the kerchief and whispered fast. "What has happened?"

"Alan is dead," Ainsley said quietly. "It is dangerous, but you must do as I ask as soon as possible. I shall be fine here."

Ms. Rielly stood. "That's it, then." She left before Pellier could stop her with any queries.

Reginald waited outside with a hansom, which she directed to the cemetery. She settled back into the cab, slipping the kerchief away. She hadn't been sure what she would do when she walked into Scotland Yard. She hadn't been sure she had heard correctly when one of Alan's informants at the Boudoir had shared what had transpired.

Alan was dead, Ainsley detained. And now, she was to go grave digging.

Swanson opened the cell door with a silent, pinched look. He said nothing as he escorted the unfortunate lord out of the detainment hall and into the main rooms of Scotland Yard. Ainsley prepared an argument to delay his finger printing.

Pellier appeared at Swanson's side. "I respectfully disagree, sir. We should not allow his release."

A voice resounded across the room. "Is Her Majesty's word not enough for you, Officer Pellier?" Michael Peighton stood in full Royal Guard attire, the medals shining severely. "I would gladly relay your concern to Her Highness, should you think it necessary."

Pellier stammered. "No, sir!" He saluted and froze in place.

Swanson made a rough noise in his throat. "You are free to go with our apologies, Sir Peighton. We did not realize you were on assignment from the High Order."

Michael stepped in. "Yes, as I explained, this man is working with me on a very sensitive case. As such, his identity and goings on are strictly confidential. You will hand over anything on the Foster incident to my jurisdiction."

Pellier was still frozen when the two men left. When they had put a safe distance between themselves and the law enforcers, Michael spoke, "I have arranged a carriage to return you to the manor. I have no idea of the location of your manservant."

"So now I am employed by you?" Ainsley asked skeptically. "And let us drop the pretense. I know you have been watching me. Surely you know Reginald's whereabouts."

Michael smiled. "You've become paranoid, Benjamin. Although, narrowly avoiding being shot can make one so. And you are welcome for keeping your record pristine."

"Please, I muddied that record as a young man." Ainsley turned to the other, halting them. "Michael. What do you know of this? What have you discerned already?"

The man appraised Ainsley and in that moment, Benjamin noticed just how much Michael had changed. The subtle lines beginning on his forehead, the hardened, unwavering blue of his irises, and the rough uniform hanging from his athletic but drooping build. Any trace of the boy he had met so long ago was buried under a tough exterior he had no doubt acquired through hardship, the first layer being donned after his sister's death.

Michael said softly but firmly, "This case may be connected to the one assigned to me. Alan, as you know, was not always friend to the most savory of characters. Please, for your houseguest's sake, try to relegate yourselves to staying within the manor. I realize Alan was a dear friend, but we of the High Order do not need you or Dr. Rielly poking into dangerous corners." At this, he smiled a little sadly.

Lord Ainsley's jaw was set with grief all over again. "Michael… I wish events had been different for you and I."

A heady silence fell, broken only by Michael's eventual, "I, as well, Benjamin."

The carriage spirited Ainsley home, the rain still falling heavily. He sighed deeply when the manor came into view. He felt sluggish, weighed down by death.

Ainsley could not shake the foreboding sense of hidden activity stirring below the surface of tonight's events. Slowly, he felt an ensemble had begun to tune their instruments, dark pages of chaotic notes splashed on pages. The maestro lifts his arms and like puppets they move. The intro is quiet and almost relaxing, like a lullaby. The pace begins to build and the overture crashes, sharp cymbals like lightning and trumpets sounding like the fall of Jericho. The maestro's hands are all fury, slashing at imagined threats. He stops suddenly but he is not out of breath. He regards his orchestra.

They have reached the crescendo.

"And just why did you feel the need to send me grave robbing of all things?"

Ainsley woke from his spell. Ms. Rielly stood in front of him plastered in mud from her ankles to her shoulders. Her dress was most certainly ruined, to say the least, and Reginald too stood in a similar state. She was tapping her foot, her hair felled and snarled.

He lifted himself from his chair. "Did you find anything?"

Reginald took up the answer as a peeved Ms. Rielly stalked off in a muddy stomp. "The rain did much to render the ground nearly impassable, but we continued on to the Ainsley plot. Seeing the graves undisturbed as they were, we thoroughly searched the area, but to no avail. Would you have me order an exhumation, sir?"

Lord Ainsley shook his head. "Clean up, Reginald, you have done more than enough."

"Sir, might I request you do the same?" Reginald gestured to his clothes. "Ms. Rielly was too upset to notice, but she may return soon."

Ainsley had only then realized he was still in the same coat Alan had died upon, his hands still painted a rusty color. "Oh."

"'Tis alright, milord. Come." Reginald guided his master. "Let us make you right, sir. You'll feel better." He reminisced silently on the days when he would take care of Ainsley as a child. As they journeyed upstairs, Reginald spoke, "There is one last thing that impeded further search of the grave, sir. I do not sense Ms. Rielly had come to the realization, but we were being watched. I am certain."

"Yes, I believe I have felt that way as of late as well," he responded. "I am not convinced that Michael does not have me under surveillance. But that shot! A rifle of some sort. We must gain access to the autopsy."

"I shall work on that, sir. Please do not think of such things yet," Reginald gave him a knowing look. "Grieve. You are allowed that much."

Ainsley sighed. "Now is not the time for allowances. I fear there is a monster orchestrating all of this just outside our door. I must attain answers now, or I never shall." He left Reginald outside his quarters and shut himself in.

Now, the crescendo.

Chapter Nine
'What's in a Name?'
Shakespeare

Three days had passed, yet it seemed like weeks. Ms. Rielly threw herself headlong into her work, experimenting long into the night until the sun had risen to put her to shame. She compared samples, ran as many tests as were available to her, and even began a trial of her own.

She could not stop or be distracted, which was well enough as anyone would have it. Ainsley had shut himself in his room and she dared not go near. She spent every hour in the theater, occasionally requesting Reginald's assistance.

"You truly are another appendage!" she marveled.

Reginald handed her a beaker, glancing at her notes. "I do appreciate the compliment. You are quite amazing yourself, Ms. Rielly. I know nothing of the sciences. Seems the moment I learn one fact, the next day there are more to learn."

"That's what is most fascinating, my dear Reginald," she did not look up as she talked. "Science is ever changing in our modern world. Ever growing. There is still so much to discover. And even create." She smiled, then reflected somberly. "Is he all right? I regret not feeling the death in the way he does. I cannot properly empathize."

"This is normal. You were not well acquainted with the gentleman before he was gone from us." He passed her a syringe. "If this is all, I should be getting lunch. Lord Ainsley seems well, but I must often remind him to eat."

She finally broke from her work. "Yes, of course. Thank you, Reginald. And tell him... I am... ahem..." she trailed off.

"I shall give him your best," Reginald assured.

She smiled and watched him go. Reginald gathered fresh tea from the kitchen and a small meal, bringing it on a silver tray to his master's thick red oak door. He tapped twice and tried as he did every day to turn the knob. Thus far, he had resorted to leaving the food and coming back later to retrieve the thankfully empty tray, the door still locked. This time, however, the handle gave way. Reginald entered and took in the cacophony of the room. Books abandoned on certain pages, maps pinned to walls, shelves emptied, trinkets of high esteem placed carefully in safer places.

Lord Ainsley stood puzzling over a hand-written book, dark circles hollowing out his eyes even more than usual. He had barely acknowledged Reginald but an open door was more than enough to encourage the butler. He set the tray atop a sheaf of papers and waited for his master's bidding.

Eventually, Ainsley asked, "How is she?"

Reginald felt comforted by his lord's wellbeing remaining intact, even if it was in a questionable state. "She is well, my lord. She thrives in her work."

"Very good." He went silent for a while again, but Reginald waited patiently. "I grieved. I read. I still read. I am going over our family history. I find retracing this quite frustrating. All my father ever recorded was his strange inspirations and thorns in his side. Business records seem a bit doctored, but nothing too unusual. I think over Alan's last words in agony, unable to discern the meaning of them. I still think I should be looking into the High Order and Michael's part in all this. He knows more than he lets on."

"Then why study the family?" Reginald interjected the question carefully, unsure if Ainsley was still speaking to him or just to himself.

"I had thought when Alan mentioned my father so close to his grave... along with buried truth. Coincidence? But then we found nothing but mud," Ainsley paced as he said all this, then stopped. "Did you say something, Reginald?"

"Just that Ms. Rielly is well, sir," he replied.

"Ah, yes. Very good." He picked up his notes. "And did she put you to work?"

"Yes, sir. Although, the important things she does herself. I cannot interpret her notes."

Ainsley sipped the now cold tea absentmindedly. "Too flowery in expression?"

"No, it appears she has her own written code," Reginald explained. "Shall I fetch hotter tea for you?"

Ainsley jolted as if awakening. "She writes in code? A code. Of course! He was speaking in code, but not of what I had assumed! Oh, my brother, you were lucid after all."

He dropped the papers and gave the teacup to Reginald, rushing away toward the theater.

Ms. Rielly was stunned when he swept in. "You've come out!"

He took her in a wild twirl of an embrace. "You write in code!" he proclaimed, swinging her about. "You, my dear, have reminded me of something I had not thought of in years!"

Ms. Rielly giggled until he set her down at last. "What is this about?"

"A code of sorts. Alan and I had invented it as a safety measure when we were in dangerous places," he spoke quickly. "He called me his brother. We had certain phrases like that. I cannot believe I had forgotten!"

"Yes, well, what does it all mean?" Ms. Rielly asked.

"We need to return to the cemetery," he said. "We shall draw out the answers! In the meantime, Reginald, how goes the other aspect?"

"The autopsy has been closed but we cannot gain access. Courtesy of the High Order," he responded.

Ainsley smiled a little. "Well, courtesy of the High Order, we shall be visiting our dear chief inspector."

Lord Ainsley strode into Scotland Yard as if he owned it and all its people, which, to them, he could have. Ms. Rielly followed closely behind, a folder and pen in her hands. The occupants of the room quickly stopped what they were doing to stare at the two.

Swanson was immediately at their side. "Sir, how may we be of service?"

"I realize Sir Peighton ordered all the records you have gathered on the Foster case be turned over. This includes the mortician's notes. I would like to see any and all records you are storing for him. Am I correct in assuming Sir Peighton has you keeping them for further reference?" Ainsley kept his eyes straight ahead.

"Yes, sir. Let me show you." The inspector led them to the records room. "My officers keep all files organized alphabetically. I can assist you, if you wish."

"We shall not be requiring your presence, chief inspector, thank you," Ms. Rielly dismissed him with a flick of her wrist. As the burly man left with a grunt, Ainsley raised an eyebrow at her and she shrugged. They set to work.

"Alphabetical, my corset!" Ms. Rielly huffed, her fingers flying deftly through boxes. "How do we know Michael hasn't confiscated all the notes?"

"A small contingent such as his, whipped together so hastily, I would not be surprised if he was using his own apartments as a headquarters. Other than that, I'm afraid we are relying on Lady Fortune." He spread out a file. "She seems to appreciate our blind trust rewardingly."

"You've found something!" Ms. Rielly leaned over to see.

Her hair smelled of lavender. Ainsley breathed her in quietly, studying her profile. He turned away. "Some of the mortician's notes and hypotheses. The shot was of .75 caliber, recovered from the body. My thoughts coincide with the weapon being of a rifle class. That may explain why I was not shot myself immediately following."

"Rifles take time to reload?" Ms. Rielly still read the notes diligently. "Why a rifle, then? Not a pistol? Something more compact with a larger magazine? You know they have been designing such a thing for some time now. Oh, don't be so shocked. I do my research."

"I am not sure I want to know how you came by such research, Ms. Rielly. I shall remember you are simply a force to be reckoned with when knowledge is the currency." He shifted his perspective and searched more boxes.

Ms. Rielly finished her assessment of the folder and set off to pick through older-looking boxes. The papers were almost damp with mold, the ink on them blurry. Her eyes scanned through until they fell on a familiar name: 'Moira Annabel Davies.'

"Oh," such a small sound through her thin lips, expressing all the truth and grief she had held back. She opened the file and read, her shoulders beginning to wrack with guilt. She'd been so distracted from the search for her friend. And now, with the truth in front of her…

Within the folder's pages, her friend's name stared back at her, the letters bold and final. She had been found in an alley, cut stem to stern with surgical precision, the modus operandi of only one killer: Jack the Ripper. Among the evidence bagged at the scene was a note left to the lead inspector, further solidifying the culprit. She felt sick and was unable to read more.

She slipped the file back in place and gazed across the room at Lord Ainsley. Benjamin. She felt a revelation take root and being to grow. She looked at him through the lens of a new understanding of their experiences together. Of his acceptance of her and the implicit trust she placed in him. She wiped away a tear and turned back to rifle through more records.

A sharp gasp made her look up. Ainsley's brow was furrowed, a file in his tight grasp. "My father. He was detained here."

"Whatever for?" Ms. Rielly wandered over to him, reading around his arm. "He stole medical supplies? I have done that before!"

Ainsley set the thin record down. "I never knew. He didn't seem the type to do something so reckless."

Ms. Rielly sighed. "We all want to believe we know our loved ones better than anyone else. No one is perfect. And it looks like your father was quite young when this transpired."

Ainsley's face was unreadable and he changed the subject. "Your studies on the blood cultures. How does it fare? Anything of note?"

Ms. Rielly threw her shoulders back proudly. "Indeed. I have been working on a groundbreaking test that may very well change the way we view blood forever! I just have a few kinks to work out. Some more research on Sir William Osler and William Hewson's work in the field. Why do you ask?"

His voice was haunted. "I have been experiencing a recurring dream of late. Part of it is surely a memory. I was in the jungles of Africa interacting with the BaBukusu. The Omukasa of the tribe warned me of a tree of great power. A tree of mouths. I was young and unafraid and I asked someone to lead me to it. In reality, the tree was normal enough, just rather large. I remember the next part as if through a fog…" His eyes closed. "I was sick. The tribesmen gathered the healers but quickly abandoned me to die. My blood, they feared, was cursed. The said the Tree of Hunger had given me a plague. Reginald said I must have been sick for weeks because when I finally returned home, I had been gone longer than expected."

"Your health improved?"

He nodded. "The tribe chief, the Omukasa, forbade me to ever return. I had almost believed all this was just a nightmare my mind had created. But I know now the expedition was real."

"That is when you came back to London a changed man," Ms. Rielly surmised. "That was the one to end your travels?"

"That, dear Ms. Rielly, was not the one to end my journeys. But yes, I was much altered. That was when I realized the darkness in my future…" He shook his head. "I am not making sense. I suppose I felt I just had to tell someone. Perhaps now the Tree of Hunger will stop haunting me… in my dreams, the tree is covered with real mouths. Each one is saying something I cannot understand."

"Please," Ms. Rielly put a hand tentatively on his, "if ever you need someone to tell these things to, I am here." He searched her, their faces not far from one another. She cleared her throat and backed up. "Do you happen to remember when you first noticed the change in your blood? How long has it been this way?"

"That is what is so confusing, Ms. Rielly. When the expedition took a wrong turn with the BaBukusu, when I fell ill, I felt as if I was discovering the oddity for the first time. And yet, some part of me felt a familiarity, as though I had, in truth, been aware of the affliction for some time. I cannot recall it ever being brought to my attention as a child, though. Surely, I must have had doctor's visits or scrapes that would have revealed the condition. So, was it a sudden illness that brought it on?"

"Please tell me you're not suddenly going to say we need to go visit a tree with mouths," Ms. Rielly winced. "Do you think the tree caused it?"

"As I've only just begun to remember the details with accuracy, I cannot be sure. But rest assured, we are not going to Africa."

She hemmed and hawed. "But if this tree is the cause, further study might yield some answers."

"We cannot, Ms. Rielly. As I am banned, I must respect the Omukasa. And also—"

"Oh, bings on him! Forget some old superstition. We may have real answers here!"

"The tree is gone, Ms. Rielly."

"What?"

"Burned in recent wars that ate up the forests." He gave a halfhearted smile. "It is quite all right. I suppose that is why I ask how your research goes. I have the utmost faith in your groundbreaking test."

She groaned. "But it's not even finished yet!"

"Still quite all right, Ms. Rielly." He dusted off his coat. "Even if I learn nothing more of my strange affliction, all will be well. I feel certain of it. In the meanwhile, we have more pressing matters to attend to." He held out a hand. "Shall we visit the dead?"

The King's Cemetery was still soggy from the recent rain, but much easier to traverse. In anticipation for this leg of their journey, Ms. Rielly had donned new boots that were laced up her calves and wore a shorter dress. She poked about behind Lord Ainsley, still reflecting on how he had taken her hand. Her face grew tight with the tell-tale rush of red and she rejoiced that Ainsley could not see.

"Here it is," Ainsley called.

He had stopped in front of a large stone with two names etched into the miserable gray. Ms. Rielly inhaled deeply and stepped forward. "Mr. and Mrs. George Connor Ainsley II. Here I meet your parents. Officially." Her heart thumped despite herself. How silly to be nervous, she thought.

"Someone else has been here recently," Ainsley stooped to inspect a smattering of foreign footprints. "Looks like they spent some time here. Maybe looking for information Alan left behind?"

"The ground remains as it was before. I see no recent digging," Ms. Rielly said.

"The size of the print and the long gait suggests a man. Do you see anything I may have overlooked, Ms. Rielly?"

She was staring across the wide expanse of graves. "This cemetery is close to where you found me that night, isn't it?"

"Do you think the locations are related?" A thought crossed his mind. "The man who drugged you... you think he may be the shooter?"

She shook her head as if shaking off a dream. "No, I'm sorry. I was just recalling. It may have nothing to do with this incident. Why would he drug me and then shoot Mr. Foster? No, perhaps... do you think this could *all* be totally unrelated?"

"What is your meaning?"

"London is a big city. I am just thinking of how I was certain you were Moira's murderer. Yet, it turned out her death was completely unrelated to you. The rumor of her going into your manor… it was unfounded. Or confused with someone else." She paused. "Mr. Foster did not always associate with the most upright fellows. Do you not think that this might have been retribution for something else?"

"Then, all these events could just be coincidence again?" Ainsley asked no one in particular. "There seem to be too many parallels. No, Ms. Rielly, I believe all of this is connected. Whatever Alan had discovered put him in danger. And to solve the mystery, we must uncover what he found."

"I remain with you all the way," she said. "Just don't suddenly start in on how all of this is too dangerous for a lady and how I should go home."

"No," he said. "I can better protect you when you are near."

She blinked, the red rushing back into place. Ainsley seemed to react, blinking back at her as if to make sure he was seeing correctly. She half expected him to rub his eyelids.

He swallowed. "I assume by your earlier words you know the outcome of your friend? And that I have hidden it for some time."

Ms. Rielly nodded. "I understand your hesitation. My search for her is complete. Perhaps in helping you I will honor her in some way. Find a way to help people like her."

"Yes, I fear her true killer is beyond our abilities," Ainsley said. "A monster the likes of which our society has yet to comprehend."

She shivered.

A noise made them both start, hearts pounding in unison. Ainsley gasped and dove, taking Ms. Rielly into his arms and to the ground. She screamed as the headstone beside her cracked, a bullet burying into the Ainsley name. There was another shot, further away, and then silence.

They breathed hard, Ainsley looking fierce, his eyes hunting. Ms. Rielly couldn't help looking straight at him, as he had literally enveloped her with his own body. She heard footsteps and her heart quickened.

"Master Ainsley? Are you well?" Reginald called out.

Ainsley helped Ms. Rielly to her feet. "Yes, thank you, Reginald. He returned just as we thought."

Ms. Rielly stammered. "We were bait?"

Reginald handed over a long-barreled rifle to Ainsley. "I could not see the shooter clearly, sir. But he dropped his weapon. I believe this is what killed Mr. Foster."

"Wait just a tick!" she demanded. "You knew we were just waiting to be shot at?"

"I would be lying if I didn't say I had hoped it would turn out like this," Ainsley admitted. "As I only half understand Alan's code, I hoped if we spent some time here, we might lure out the culprit. I apologize for putting you in danger. Perhaps you would have preferred to stay at home?"

"Don't. You. Start," she growled.

"We shall be able to determine much from this weapon," Ainsley hefted it expertly. "Already I can say the owner only meant to shoot one person today."

"Is it hard to reload, as we thought?" Ms. Rielly was still angry but too curious to allow it to tamp down the many questions buzzing through her mind.

"Indeed, Ms. Rielly." He smiled. "This is a very specific and very talkative gun. This is a Baker Rifle."

Ms. Rielly raised an eyebrow speculatively. "I know I may have some modern knowledge, but I am a woman of knives, in the end. Now tell me, should this name mean something to me? Other than almost being the cause of my death?"

"What's in a name?" Ainsley mused. "Let us find out."

Ms. Rielly huddled under a quilt, curled up on a lavish chair by the fireplace. She still felt the adrenaline rushing through her from her near-death experience. She knew Ainsley would never have allowed her to be harmed, but he risked himself without a second thought. She would not let herself think of if the bullet had struck him.

"We've finished." Ainsley joined her, seating himself. "Reginald and I have compared everything carefully, but we now know all there is about this particular Baker."

"I take it we are not speaking of a maker of sweets?"

He smiled, something she noticed him doing more frequently.

"The Baker Rifle is an infantry gun. It was first produced by a man named Ezekiel Baker. But what really matters is that this gun was likely owned by a soldier, most likely during the Napoleonic War. We are researching the rosters now. We may be able to track the gun to its owner."

"We may not need to do so much work, Master Ainsley," Reginald carried the gun in gloved hands. "Perhaps we can take advantage of Sir Peighton's kindness once again? I can deliver the gun posthaste."

"Yes, good thinking. Please do so at once," Ainsley decided.

Ms. Rielly protested. "Michael will never share any information he finds with us."

"We do not mean to deliver it to Sir Peighton," the butler amended. "We shall give it to Chief Inspector Swanson."

She smiled, suddenly in on the plan. "He shall be ever eager to assist one of the High Order."

***

Benjamin could still envision that fateful day. He held Jane close and promised to love her forever. Sun shone off the glossy locks of her hair. She pulled the ribbons from her sleeves, laughing. And then she was gone.

A thick, hot jungle closed around him. Vines wound around his leg and branches clawed at his face. A tree was groaning, leaning toward him. The bark split into thousands of mouths, their lips moving as one. They grew in volume, scared and angry, all saying the same thing:

"Poison! Plague! Disease! We are hungry for ambition!"

A mouth bit his arm and black oozed out.

He cried out soundlessly into the night, his mind racing and hands clenched from the hallucinated fight. He clawed at where the tree had bitten him. The dream was already fading. His chest tightened, his fingers wet.

He had struck his arm on something in his sleep and now it bled. He breathed slower, attempting to calm himself, but his chest throbbed. He heard a knock on his door.

Reginald entered. "Sir, are you feeling well?"

Ainsley's heart pounded within. "What is it? Is Ms. Rielly alright?"

"I delivered the Baker as you requested. The Yard shall contact us as soon as they have the roster." Reginald dropped the business-like tone, back to his concern, "Sir, are you getting enough sleep? You must remember yourself."

"I'm fine," Ainsley could not think. He kept hearing the Tree of Hunger in his ears. The mouths hid beneath every blink, every closing of his eyes showed them on the back of his eyelids.

'Death!' they cried.

Chapter Ten

Of Two Men

Morning arrived and Reginald served breakfast. Ms. Rielly was disheveled, roused early, and already fuming. Lord Ainsley was brooding. The Yard had taken no time at all to deliver the roster for which they searched. But alas, the answer only served to create more questions.

"I cannot make sense of it," Ms. Rielly was mumbling. "Are you sure the name has no connection?"

The roster had yielded the name of the owner, but no one in the Ainsley household knew of him. It was random and did not fit, until Lord Ainsley reached the most logical conclusion:

"The roster has been forged," Ainsley said. "And I know by whom. Michael."

Ms. Rielly practically growled. "Why must he poke his nose into this?"

"He wants to halt whatever investigation we may be doing," he said. "Michael knows we are meddling in dangerous areas."

"Does he know what we are doing?"

"That is precisely what you are going to find out," Ainsley sighed. "I didn't want to do this, but we must ascertain the truth about the rifle. If Michael has any information, it will be within his quarters. Yet, somehow I doubt he will allow me the opportunity."

"I will do it," Ms. Rielly nodded. "He won't suspect me."

"You must go with Reginald, of course. He will create a diversion to give you the time to search. You must be quick and take great care not to leave anything out of place." Ainsley placed a hand on her shoulder. "You will be safe. I loathe to admit it, but Michael's quarters are perhaps the safest place for you to be."

"I will find what we need, Lord Ainsley." She squared her jaw. "Now then, let us arm me to the teeth!"

Sir Peighton was quite surprised to see Ms. Rielly and her escort at his door, but recovered quickly and let them inside. "What brings you here, Jekyllyne?"

"I regret how impulsive I am at times, Michael," she said. "I felt the need for some company other than those at the manor. Please wait outside the room, Reginald," she ordered as they sat in the tearoom.

"Yes, ma'am," Reginald bowed and took up his post.

Michael sat. "I must admit after our last exchange, I feared you would never grace these rooms again. I must apologize once again for my behavior."

"Worry not, Michael. It is forgotten," Ms. Rielly smiled. "Shall we have tea?" The time it would take to make a brew might afford her some exploration.

"Ah, it is well enough! I have just made a fresh pot before you rang." Michael jumped up and was bringing the tea before Ms. Rielly could think twice. "I do hope it is to your liking."

He poured tea into a delicate cup, which she sipped with practiced daintiness. "It is wonderful." In actuality, she did not taste the tea as her mind was too preoccupied. How to move this conversation toward his study? Then, clarity. "Last time I was here, you spoke of how refreshing it was to recall your sister with someone. I must confess, I have been thinking often of your sister. Do you happen to have any photos of her within your study?"

Michael deliberated for a moment, as if still processing her request. "Yes. I do. Please come with me." He took her hand and led her to a room off the great hall. They passed Reginald and Ms. Rielly winked.

His study was the polar opposite of Ainsley's. Every object had a place and every place had an object, but nothing was out of order. His desk held pristine stacks of folders that were no doubt alphabetized, his pens were straightened, and not a drop of ink had fallen to the shiny wood finish. His shelves were sparse, but what books he did have were large with titles that were beyond even Ms. Rielly's plethora of knowledge. A window was open and flowers from a hanging box tipped lazily inside, providing a sweet scent with each breeze. There was an oversized, relaxed chair in one corner with a book bisected by the arm, waiting to be resumed.

Michael went to the desk and, from a small leather-bound journal in a drawer, retrieved the photo Ms. Rielly had inquired of. "Here. She's the one on the left."

Ms. Rielly held the snapshot with her fingertips. It was a fragile thing, black and white and very old. Next to the woman he had pointed to, Ms. Rielly could discern

Michael's own likeness in a rather young boy standing in front of another woman she guessed to be his mother.

Jane Peighton was stunning. Her eyes were bright and her smile beaming. Her tiny hands were on Michael's shoulder, her body angled toward him protectively. Michael's own smile mirrored hers so exactly it was impossible not to see the resemblance.

"She's beautiful," Ms. Rielly felt a pang in her breast. Surely not jealousy for a woman long dead? Perhaps it was, but she recognized it also as grief. "I can see the love she had for you plainly."

Michael smiled. "Thank you. You do not know it, but we had different fathers. Even though there easily was enough to separate us forever, she would not allow it. She treated me no differently, even though she did not feel the same affection toward my father."

"I had no idea." She handed the photo back gingerly. "She must have been quite the amazing woman."

"Yes, but I'm afraid that was her downfall," he said. "It takes quite an amazing woman to grab an Ainsley's eye. And that she did."

Ms. Rielly tried to halt her mind from deciphering his meaning, but he continued.

"I hope the same fate will not befall you. I know I am too late to shield you from his gaze, but perhaps I can protect you from his tendency to drag young girls through danger." Michael took her hands in his. "Please, do you know anything about what he's doing? Do you know why he is using you to gain access to medical files?"

She looked away. "He just wants to know what happened to his friend."

"But we both know there is more to it than that. You two have been popping up all over. And not just with my cousin's body." He held her hands tight. "Why was he at the Torso Killer's crime scene? Surely you must be worried by now. His acquaintances keep dying, Jekyllyne. How does that bode for you?"

Ms. Rielly was desperate for Reginald's diversion. Michael knew much more than they had thought, but why? Why was he investigating Lord Ainsley?

"Do you think he's the one killing them?" she asked incredulously.

"I think he is hiding something from all of us. And I won't allow him to harm another woman that I care for."

Ms. Rielly broke his grasp. "What—"

They both started as a crash echoed from the great hall. Michael ran from the room to discern the origin and Ms. Rielly took her chance. She let her fingers fly over the pages on his desk as quickly as she could, her eyes searching so frantically that they gave her a headache. She had to find the owner of the rifle, but the desk seemed to hold no answers. She glanced over to the drawer from which the photo had come and made a quick determination to search there.

Michael's voice grew louder and she composed herself before he came in. He was ruffled but smiling. "Poor chap, your butler fell quite asleep standing up. He fell into my vase and made a right mess of it. Fortunately, he wasn't harmed."

"I should be going now, Michael," Ms. Rielly declared. "I apologize for my butler's inadequacy. I shall order him some rest immediately." She moved to the door.

"I am glad you visited me, Jekyllyne," Michael said. "I too apologize for letting my work turn our conversation sour."

"Quite forgiven, Michael. I had forgotten that you were related to the recently deceased. Surely you are still grieving," she said. "Fortunate of you to recover the weapon. I'm confident it will lead you to the killer."

"What weapon?"

Ms. Rielly's heartbeat stilled. "I heard Scotland Yard was the recipient of an anonymous donation, a gun they believed to be the killer's. Wouldn't they have passed it off to you?"

"They would have, if there was any such gun," Michael said. "But as there isn't, we are still investigating what we can. Odd. Who did you hear such a rumor from?"

"Ms. Rielly, shall we go?" Reginald appeared at her arm.

"Yes, Reginald. Let us go." She shook her head. "I must have been mistaken, Michael. Thank you for having me on such short notice. I'll try to send a post first next time."

"There will be a next time, then?"

"Perhaps."

"I must acquire some items, Lord Ainsley."

Ms. Rielly approached him a few days after the visit with Sir Peighton. She had told him upon her return from his mission that she was unable to find anything of relevance for lack of time. Reginald apologized for not creating a better distraction, but she waved it off quickly, more focused on returning to her work in the theatre.

"Of what items do you speak?" He raised an eyebrow.

"I have gone as far as I can with the options you have provided, but I am afraid I must do something that has never been done; I must invent the item I need. To do that, I need to visit some contacts of mine in the underbelly of London."

"Assure me it will have nothing to do with a body and I shall acquiesce," he said.

"I assure you," she smiled.

"Then I shall send Reginald forthwith."

"No, I was rather thinking I would feel better with you." She tried not to blush. "There are things I'd like to show you. Alone."

She delighted in the detection of reddening in his face when he agreed. If he did not read into her implications, then it would be harder to do what she needed to. After all, who better than her to reveal a conspiracy?

"Two birds with one stone, I tell you! That is what we are doing this day!" Ms. Rielly walked jovially, Ainsley trailing behind.

"I've still not come to understand what exactly the second bird is, Ms. Rielly," he said.

"Oh, quit with the sour puss!" she commanded. "We are to see an old friend of mine and he won't stand for anything but smiles in his abode!"

"Interesting abode," Ainsley commented when they had arrived at a business marked 'Undertaker—we build every "body" a home.'

The entrance creaked and shed a cloud of dust as they ventured in. The room was dark and smelled of chemicals. There were coffins of varying sizes leaning against the walls and vases large enough to house a body decorated the open spaces. Ms. Rielly was accustomed to winding through the

Undertaker's particular furnishings, but the larger Lord Ainsley shouldered through nervously, trying to avoid knocking over one of the vases.

"The man we are meeting is a peculiar one, but he is well travelled and can often procure oddities others cannot."

"Well, is that not the truth? 'Peculiar' is a good word for one such as myself," a man stepped forward seemingly from nowhere. Even in the dim light his long tied-back hair shone red. "An Irish undertaker in England."

"There is much more peculiarity about you than your heritage, Ronan," Ms. Rielly smiled at the man as he wrapped an arm round her petite frame.

"You look well! I was worried, you know! You haven't been by for practice in some time." He let her go and chuckled. "Used to be not a week went by without you coming to dissect one of my patrons."

"Ronan… this is Lord Ainsley of Ainsley Manor." Ms. Rielly blushed and hoped he could not see in the dark.

Ainsley nodded. "I am pleased to make the acquaintance of someone who knows our dear Ms. Rielly."

Ronan laughed. "No need to stand on ceremony then! Have you been taking good care of her?"

She interrupted for fear of her face beginning to glow. "Yes! Ah, we are here for some items. I need some glass instruments, if you would. And… a quiet place."

Ronan's expression changed. "Yes. If you have a list, I will see if I have what you need after I lend that place."

She handed him a piece of paper. "Thank you, Ronan."

"This way," he said, leading them both to a closed coffin among those on the wall. "You should be able to talk in here."

Ainsley was about to point out the difficulty in logistics of two people discussing anything contained within a casket when Ronan moved the lid across to reveal an opening. They stepped through into a smaller room with a clean table and many shelves stocked with liquids unknown. Presumably, this was where the undertaker worked, not only on preparing the coffins, but the bodies as well. The lid of the door was shut between them and Ronan, seeming to suck the air from the room.

"What is this about, Ms. Rielly?" Ainsley asked.

"I apologize for bringing you here to discuss this, but I fear the manor is not the right place. Yes, I needed some items only Ronan would have for the scope I am inventing, but his rooms were also the ideal place for an unfortunate conversation." She turned to him. "I believe Reginald has betrayed you."

"Betrayed me?"

"Yes," Ms. Rielly expounded. "I told you that I had found nothing in Sir Peighton's room and that much was true. What I did find was in conversation. Michael knew nothing of the rifle. He said Scotland Yard had never received the weapon and seemed genuinely confused with my questions. His confusion coincides with the fact that in none of his papers on the case did I find any mention of the Baker Rifle. The most likely conclusion then would be that Reginald did not deliver the rifle at all."

"You're saying then that Reginald was the one to forge the roster?" Ainsley crossed his arms over his chest.

She took a deep breath. "Yes. I am sincerely suspicious that he forged the documents and hid the rifle. I tried not to let on that I had discovered anything, should he have been listening to my conversation with Michael, but I knew I had to tell you somehow."

"Why would he do this?"

"I don't know, but I hope I am wrong. Really, I do. You know how I am fond of him, but nothing else makes sense." She put a hand on his.

"I know. I just don't understand why he would interfere. I shall have to deal with this carefully." His fingers closed over hers unbeknownst to himself, the other hand going to his forehead. "Our last lead was that rifle."

Ms. Rielly bit her lip, tugging her sleeve. "Look, I know this turns our plans a bit on their heads, but if Ronan has everything I need, then what I am about to do is going to alter the course of history. And if it works, we will know everything about your blood. You will finally know how your blood became like this."

Suddenly she became very aware of how close Ainsley was and how his hand felt in hers. For once, she didn't feel the need to replace the contact with the cold steel of her scalpel. For once she wished with all her being that it would last.

She waited in the stifling silence for him to break away, to speak and at once free her from that spot, but no such moment came. Benjamin shifted a little closer and her lower back bumped against the table. There was no mistaking his intentions now. She dared look up and met his black stare, her breath quickening. Her thoughts flashed back to Michael and she banished them in disgust. Michael had been wrong about Benjamin, she was sure of it. He would never harm her. She would not catch herself thinking of one man whilst in the arms of another!

"I don't know how to tell you this…" he began, his lips inches from hers. "But you have a cockroach in your hair." She gasped and he pinned her. "It's okay! I almost have it." He pulled away from her body, something unnamable in his fingers, and she squeaked with repulsion. "There." He released the insect and she jerked as far from where it landed as possible, practically landing in Ainsley's arms.

He laughed and she burned with fury. "You think that is funny? UGH! How horrid! And in my hair!" she lamented, her fingers combing through her locks for more hidden beasts.

"Thank you, Llyne!" he said between catching his breath and laughing. "Really. For trying to comfort me, in your own way."

"What, you think I put that thing in my hair on purpose?" She shook out her dress.

"No, no. For everything else." He smiled. "For staying. Even after you had found your friend."

She stopped. "Of course I stayed. But I want you to understand it is not because we had a deal. And it isn't even because your blood is so intriguing."

Ainsley asked. "Then why?"

She smiled softly. "Well, I am figuring that out as I go, myself. But I think it has to do with you calling me Llyne just now. I think I'd like to believe we are friends."

He blinked hard. "I did call you that, didn't I? How strange, it was like second nature. I take it you don't mind."

"I suppose it will do. After all, it's better than Jekyllyne. And Benjamin is much better than LORD Ainsley," she explained. "I hope… you won't object?"

Benjamin smiled. "That's what friends do, yes?"

132

Chapter Eleven

'Keep Your Friends Close...'
Sun Tzu

"Whatever am I to do with you, Reginald?" Ms. Rielly asked, hands on her hips. "Where are the drug papers?"

"You'll have to be more specific, I'm afraid. The lab is in shambles since you've returned," Reginald was already sifting, trying to help her locate them.

"The ones, you know, with the studies and cultures of my blood after I was drugged!" She sighed in exasperation, papers flying.

Ainsley watched with humor dancing across his face, his hands at work with some trinket, his legs propped up on a table full of Jekyllyne's recently acquired items. Confronting Reginald regarding his possible betrayal had been delayed, partly due to his own hesitation. Reginald must have had a reason to rid them of the gun. Until Ainsley could ascertain just what that was, he let Ms. Rielly drag him to and from the theatre.

"Three pairs of eyes would work better than two, Benjamin!" Jekyllyne chided, flurrying about.

"The addition of my eyes would only impede your swift progress, dear Llyne," he teased lightly, half paying attention.

"Here it is!" she shouted in triumph, raising the prize aloft. She brought it down, scanning it quickly then rushing to her chemicals. She began to mix some together into a concoction, holding it up to the light and making more than one sample with varying degrees of the same ingredients. She muttered to herself, scribbling in her shorthand, her eyes flashing from paper to the liquid. She loaded some into a syringe and studied it with a small smile. "Found you."

"What is it?" Curiosity had won out as Ainsley dropped his legs from the desk and stood.

"A sedative of sorts. I believe I have procured the particular hallucinogen from my night of flight," she answered. "Although its primary use may be something else entirely," she pondered. "Further study is required!" She pushed past him, in her own world again.

Ainsley sighed, reseating himself. His fingers moved with familiar deftness over the projector, setting into place the part he had been working on. He stood, flitting from lantern to lantern, silencing the flames until all was dark.

"Light tends to help my cause more than you do, Benjamin!" Rielly snapped.

"Just a moment."

There was an audible click and a light beamed through the dust. A small picture, grainy and brown, touched the wall along the far side. It moved very slightly, a pony trotting back and forth.

Jekyllyne gasped. "Moving! I've never seen anything like it!"

"This is just what has been done so far in America," Ainsley spoke. "But there is more. At least, there was."

The pony dancing on the wall fell away, the reel clipping round and round. Reginald brought the lamps back to life, respectfully bowing to his hunched over master. Rielly went to his side.

"Those pictures were beautiful." She put a hand on his arm. "Still beautiful after so many years in the shadows. I know it is hard to return to something so precious, so fragile. You fear breaking the fantasy you built around it. You fear failing it. But I hope, one day, you'll share it with me again."

Reginald had discreetly left, only to return moments later. "Sir, there is a letter. From Sir Peighton." He handed over a letter bearing an official seal of wax.

"Oh, the gobber!" Ms. Rielly crossed her arms. "What could he possibly write?"

Ainsley flipped open the seal and regarded the letter. "He requests Reginald and I meet with him."

"Just you two?" she asked.

"It is a formal request," he reiterated. "We must go. And further, you must stay here, Ms. Rielly." She began to protest, but Ainsley stopped her. "I want you here. We won't be long, but I'd prefer you go down to the lab and stay there until we return."

She gave up each line of argument running through her head and sighed in resignation. "I should really work on my tests anyway. Just don't let him leave without answers, Reginald."

"Good," Ainsley said. "Let's leave as soon as possible. The sooner our business with Peighton is concluded, the better."

"'Formal request,'" Ms. Rielly muttered to herself over her microscope, "'You'll be safe here.' I'll probably die from the sheer amount of mold in here!" She sighed. "What could Michael want?"

Ms. Rielly looked around at all the dusting trinkets, decaying props, and the broken projector.

"Is all this for her?" A twinge of jealousy twisted inside her chest. "Is not only Michael, but Ainsley too, doing this all for her?" She shook her head, banishing the thoughts.

She went back to her microscope, determined to be done with her wallowing. She leaned in to line up the sight and gasped. Her eyes squinted. "This is it!" She jumped up. "I've done it!"

Sir Michael Peighton stood at attention as Lord Ainsley joined him in the offices of his apartment. "Please sit down, Benjamin." Michael followed suit and continued, "I've summoned you and your butler for one reason. I won't beat about it. I have heard of your scuffle in the cemetery. Would you like to explain to me why you have gone against my orders? Your butler shot a weapon in London. Not to mention, your fraud with Chief Inspector Swanson. I am not pleased. How many more times will you place everyone in danger?"

Ainsley's mind worked fast behind a face that gave away nothing. "I am not entirely sure of what you speak, Sir Peighton. I believe it was you who first constituted the fraud with the Chief Inspector."

"I was giving you a chance, Benjamin!" He grew emotional, no longer able to control what he had felt for so long. "I thought it a show of good faith. But I should have known you'd take advantage! All you have ever done is take!" He bit his tongue.

Lord Ainsley took a breath. "So this is it. The final confrontation, at last? Should I request Reginald leave us?"

A pained look crossed Michael's face. "Perhaps this is it then, Lord Ainsley. You have obviously known it was coming."

"Yes," he sighed. In that one word, years of grief and disappointment resurfaced. "An apology will never suffice for my inability to save Jane."

"Tell me what happened," Michael said, teeth clenched.

Ainsley looked at him and at last saw the boy he remembered. Young, grieving, and angry. "We were in England, Michael."

"No," he shook his head. "You had taken her on some fruitless adventure to further capture her heart. They delivered the body back to us."

"To America. On an English ship," Ainsley said gently. "We were going to leave, but I convinced her she did not need to see the world. That I no longer needed to because she was my world," Ainsley paused, his heart swelling. "We disembarked from the ship and returned home. To the manor. That... is where she fell."

He blinked back visions of her unmoving body, lying where she had dropped to the ground. Around him, his theater grew quiet and cold. He held her for hours, his fantasy crumbling around him. His world had died.

"I can attest to the truthfulness of this, Sir Peighton," Reginald said.

Tears ran down Michael's face. "My sister. You didn't protect her."

Ainsley had long since dried of his own tears. His eyes stung but nothing came. "I know."

Two words: all he could express. There were no others. Ainsley only then realized that all the years he had spent blaming himself, suffering her death over and over, Michael had been experiencing the same. He did not expect forgiveness.

Michael placed his hands on Ainsley's shoulders, next to him now. He looked into his eyes. "I cannot hang onto this vendetta against you. It will be the death of me. But you cannot keep going this way! You must stop the hunt. Stay out of my business and do not drag Ms. Rielly into this!" He held out something small and shining. "I found this among the things my mother sent back eventually."

Ainsley set eyes on the diamond ring he had given to her.

"Our mother was never close to me. I always favored my father. She had not told me your intentions," Michael said. "Benjamin, I cannot forgive you for what occurred, but I cannot hate you for wanting to bring my sister happiness. Take this and don't make the same mistakes. I fight everyday not to."

Ainsley stood, the ring held gently in his fingers, a clarity in his heart. "Thank you, Michael."

Michael cleared his throat, the tears gone. "Please heed my warning. We have been tracking some of Alan Foster's old partners. He may have been working with a very dangerous group, Benjamin. Thieves, mostly. Grave diggers."

"He was selling things on the black market?"

"Worse. To a third party we've been attempting to apprehend for years. Their leader is called the Progenitor. He has his hands in everything, amassing extensive properties for himself. His group is extremely dangerous," Michael said.

"Do you think it was this connection that led to his murder?" Ainsley probed.

At this Michael's brow furrowed. "We've been assuming so. But that isn't what matters, Benjamin. If the Progenitor had anything to do with the butchery that was Madame Tusor's death, do you imagine he'll have more mercy toward Lady Rielly if she gets too close?"

Ainsley suddenly grew agitated. "I will not allow her to come to harm."

"Of course," Michael said. "I am sure you said the same of Jane. Do not think your arrogance can protect you. If I sense anything amiss, I will not hesitate to arrest you. Jekyllyne would be safer in my custody in any case."

Ainsley headed for the door. "That will not be necessary. I think we are done here. Thank you for the ring. I will send Ms. Rielly your regards."

Chapter Twelve

'With the Spilt-Out Blood of the Rose-Red Wine.'
Oscar Wilde

'This discovery will surely change the world of medicine and biology! I have created a new and enhanced way to examine blood! And oh, the things I have seen now!

'The repercussions of this discovery… my mind is boggled! Answers once closed off to us have suddenly become available! As if the waters of knowledge now flow free!

'But alas, with such a wide scope now available, I know how sick Ainsley truly is. His cells are degrading over time. At this rate he would be soon experiencing the unavoidable side effects: dizziness, heart palpitations, confusion, even hallucinations… And if I'm correct about the current state of his cells, then he already knows. And what's more, he's known from the beginning…'

Ms. Rielly shook her head, a pang in her breast. She bit her lip fiercely, determined not to break into tears. She hit the table, repeatedly, until her hand could take no more. She slumped down, catching a sob in her throat.

"How? How can I fix this?"

She heard movement upstairs and swallowed hard, collecting herself as Ainsley came down the stairs.

He noticed her disquiet immediately. "Are you well?"

"When were you going to tell me?" She tried not to clench her teeth. "You've known? That you were dying? This whole time. You could have told me what I was to expect. Instead, you blindside me. Every time."

He took a deep breath. "I have wronged you. I apologize."

She waited. "That's all? You have wronged me. You have wronged me?" She whirled on him, throwing her tiny fists at his chest. "HOW? You do not understand!" The tears came despite her attempts to hold them back.

Ainsley was shocked at her sudden outburst but let her continue. His eyes filled with the weighty truth of his own mortality, something he hadn't allowed himself to feel for some time. He could not resist, he grabbed her wrists and pulled her close, wrapping himself around her.

She gasped, her face streaked with trails of pain. "NO! Let me go! I have had enough!" She pushed him violently away. "I am done with these secrets! And your manipulations!" She ran from the basement, shoving past Reginald, and shut herself in her room.

Reginald descended to Ainsley. "I am sure she just needs time."

"She is right. I should have told her from the beginning, but it is too late now," he lamented. "I fear I will lose all of you no matter how I struggle."

"I shall always be at your side, Master Ainsley," Reginald bowed. "She needs time, I assure you."

Ainsley sighed, his eyes roving over to the projector, the ghost of his dream. He could barely feel Jane's presence among the room and all its accoutrements. Was it over by the table or by the stairs where he had held her lifeless form?

Somehow the room had changed without him noticing. There was a newly familiar spice amid the basement dust and beakers atop stacks of books recently pulled from their perches. Perhaps, they all needed time. A luxury Ainsley no longer had.

Reginald let his fingers brush his master's arm. "Sir, I advise against continuing any further. I recognize the next actions you may take and must agree with Sir Peighton. This hunt is becoming too dangerous."

"Madame Tusor may have come up against trouble of Alan's making. Whatever we are to find out, the Progenitor is where we must go," Ainsley declared. "I will not let Lorri's life go to waste. Nor Alan's. Are you still at my side, Reginald?"

Reginald bowed. "Of course, Master Ainsley."

The Lion's Boudoir was permanently low-lit, the music quiet and the alcohol strong. There was a long bar at one end of the main room and tables built into alcoves along the back. The walls were painted the colors of desire and cracking slightly. Women lounged on sofas clad in fur and propped up with pillows, eyes tracking potential patrons like a cat with a mouse.

Ainsley ordered Reginald to watch Ms. Rielly at the manor like a hawk, preferring to initially do this on his own, but not unarmed. From his business days, he was accustomed to entering rooms in which he did not belong so he carried his trusty pistol. Even so, he felt unease. Alan's partners were expecting him.

A scantily clad woman with a large wig of curls approached. She wasn't altogether stand-offish in her looks, save for the dark circles under her heavily lidded eyes. "'Ello, 'andsome. Might you spare a coin for a thirsty poor 'un? Make it worf ya while," she winked, pursing her layer of lipstick.

"Of course, my dear." He procured a shilling from somewhere amidst the tangle of hair, an old trick Alan had taught him. "Come, we'll take care of you." His mind flashed back to Ms. Rielly's deceased friend.

The woman giggled, her eyes lighting up. She poked a finger to the tip of her nose like she smelled something and sat down next to Ainsley. "You'se a good 'un. I can tell." She held up a hand, cueing the bartender. "What you doin' in the shadowy places, 'andsome?"

He could only imagine how Ms. Rielly had handled this place. He envisioned her running from woman to woman, pestering with questions, researching any way she could help them, only to get a boot squarely placed. Reginald probably had an interesting time keeping her reined in. Not to mention the prospects she probably was offered, by patron and employee alike. He almost smiled.

"I'm looking for someone. A beneficiary, perhaps. Of this place?" Ainsley asked. "Do you know of anyone who might fit?"

"You'se not talkin' 'bout the owner, eh?" She grinned, revealing missing teeth. "Told you I could tell. Good 'un."

As the bartender came to deliver drinks, the woman whispered into his ear. He handed the cups over to the girl and nodded. She stood, the wine sloshing red over the side.

"Us go somewhere quiet, yeah?" she said, leading Ainsley behind the bar and into a smaller room in the back.

There was one painted over window with tattered maroon curtains and a large lounger with an indent in the middle, leaking bits of stuffing from the sides. Although he questioned the safety of sitting, the woman insisted sweetly. She then disappeared.

Minutes passed. Ainsley shifted uncomfortably, unable to tell if he had been put on or not. The note he had sent forthwith had been answered by someone he assumed had known Alan. But perhaps it was a set up after all. The waters were churning; were there sharks?

A woman stumbled in, entirely different from the one before. She was laughing as if she had just heard a joke, her robe askew. Her shoulders were bare and pale, but not unhealthy. There was a flush to her cheeks that seemed natural and her eyes had a beautiful, entrancing sparkle. She sat on Ainsley's lap, wrapping her arms round his neck.

"Hello, love."

Ainsley was taken aback, unsure how to respond to such a creature. "Madame, I think there has been a mistake."

"No mistake, Lord Ainsley." She tilted her head, jasmine wafting from her golden locks. "Although, you're to be disappointed, as I am not the Progenitor." She slid away from him in one fluid motion, like she was one with the shadows of the room. "I am the owner of The Lion's Boudoir. Calliope." She crossed her arms over her chest. "How may I help your lordship?"

Ainsley stood. "You're aware of what I seek. I need to find the Progenitor."

"You can't," she said simply. "You're already getting too cozy with his channels. What does a man like you want with the Progenitor?"

"A friend of mine was killed and I want to know for sure he was behind it."

"Alan was unfortunate. The Progenitor did not foresee his death and mourns over his loss, just as you do. No, Alan was a casualty of something much larger and much older." She swung her hip out, adjusting her stance.

"And my other friend? The Madame?"

"Also a casualty of the same war, I'm afraid," she sighed languorously. "But I've said too much. For your sake, I believe this concludes our conversation. You know, 'sins of the father,' and what not."

Ainsley's heart jumped. "What do you mean?"

She deliberated, delighted by her own prowess. "For that, you'll have to pay."

Ainsley was about to inquire of her price but she moved before he could, pressing her lips to his. He gasped, the assault leaving his skin tainted by her makeup. She pushed him away.

"I can't give you the Progenitor, but perhaps I am bored. Perhaps I just like you. Thus, I will tell you that you are not the first Ainsley the Progenitor has had dealings with." Her cloying teases were suddenly gone, replaced by a much more serious woman. "Whether or not this information brings you peace, do not pull at the Progenitor's threads. Find your answers and bury them. The Progenitor wants nothing to do with your family name any longer."

Ainsley thanked her. "Your time has been invaluable."

She smiled, cat-like. "I hope this is not the last time we are able to trade. Alan was a close companion of mine. Perhaps you'll do as a nice replacement?"

He bowed slightly, kissing her hand. "I fear the honor is too great, my Lady Calliope."

As he left, the woman narrowed her gaze. "Perhaps… all roads must converge eventually." She pulled a glinting necklace from between her breasts, a rose gold locket on the end, dingy with age. She grinned slyly.

Ms. Rielly had been pacing non-stop, exhausted but stubborn. She couldn't leave her work the way it was. She had to know if she could deliver what Ainsley had clearly brought her there for: a cure. But her heart clashed with her mind.

"Does he expect me to just forgive him?" Her thoughts were racing. "The way he just grabbed me like that? What does he expect?" Her face burned and she squeezed her sides, remembering just how his arms felt. "You gammy dolt! Why'd you push him?"

A knock startled her, but Reginald's soft voice came. "May I enter?"

She bid him welcome, collapsing to the bed with exasperation. "You've done your part in this, too, Reginald! You knew how bad he was."

Reginald seated himself next to her. "My lady, we did not know if you would even be able to discern that much. Lord Ainsley brought you here because of your abilities, but even he was not certain anything would come of it. If you had not been able to break through as you have, he would have sent you on your way, none the wiser to his condition. He felt that was best."

"So if I had failed, he would have forced my departure? He would never have told me he was sick." She grasped the coverlet in frustration. "No matter... none of it matters. Anymore."

The butler smiled warmly. "You have indeed exceeded his expectations. Many of them."

She blushed again, eyeing the ceiling. "That doesn't change the fact that I still have to cure him. And I have no idea where to start."

"I am sure you will think of a way," he reassured her. "You are a very resourceful young woman."

"In the meantime, what do we do?"

Reginald pulled her up. "May I suggest speaking with my lord? I am sure he is concerned for your well-being."

She groaned. "Yes, of all people he worries for me, rather than himself. The one who is sick."

"I shall gather dinner," Reginald said. "Lord Ainsley should return by the evening."

"Wait, he left?" Ms. Rielly balked. "Without you? When there is a killer on the loose? And he worries for me! I'll strangle him should he return safely!"

The door closed and Ms. Rielly went to scribble on her pages.

Chapter Thirteen
And with What Loyalty Comes the Blow?

"What are your symptoms?"

"I told you, there are none."

"Benjamin…" Ms. Rielly warned.

"Headaches. Like the one I have right now in front of me."

She ignored him. "And tell me again where you went?"

"The Lion's Boudoir. To pay my respects to Alan."

"Mm-hm." She raised an eyebrow. "So you didn't find out anything new? Anything that could help us solve the murders? I thought maybe because Alan had friends at the Boudoir…"

"Not as many as you might think," Ainsley deflected. "Really, just a personal errand."

"Well, you could have chosen a better time." She paused. "Have you decided how to speak to Reginald? We have to find out what he did with the rifle if we are to ascertain our next move."

"I will. There may be nothing else I can do." He looked into her eyes as she examined him. "You just continue to perform as always, Llyne. I have faith that you will find a cure."

She blinked, avoiding his intense stare. "I will do my utmost."

"Good. Then I need your help elsewhere." He led her into a small alcove off his study, a closet of sorts. "I am beginning to think I missed something in going through my father's old business records. I could use another sifter."

"What am I searching for?" Her fingers were already picking through the files.

"Anything out of the ordinary. Numbers that don't quite add up," he said. "Alan may still have been onto something with his last words."

"Did paying your respects renew this challenge?"

"Very much so."

The tree was speaking again, only this time in slivers of intonation. The fog parted as Benjamin moved through it, the mouths waiting for him. They all moved independently, their words all different but very familiar.

Conversations he had had with people. Alan, Reginald, Jane... Then, from the chorus came his father's voice. A memory long lost.

"Father! You're back!" Little Benjamin ran into the elder's arms, noticing the way he winced. "Are you all right?"

His father's lack of answer was not what perturbed him the most, but rather it was the way he looked at him. Like a man of regret, suffering under a weight only he could bear. Now, as he stood in front of the tree of mouths, Benjamin watched the scene play out before him. Watched how his father hid the pain.

"What have you done?" Ainsley wondered. "Were you working with the Progenitor my whole childhood? What were you doing for him? What was he doing for you?"

The trees grew silent. One voice spoke. It was Jekyllyne.

"Where have you gone this time?" She laughed, her eyes squinting. "Are you in Africa? Mumbai? I've had enough of your going off on your own! You can't keep me from danger my whole life!"

The tree morphed and she was there, in its place. She wore the dress he had made for her for the ball at Almack's. The way she held out her arms, welcoming, took his breath away.

"Don't try to protect me. Don't keep anything more from me," she begged. "I cannot take much more; the way you look at me. The way you hold me. So I'm going to find out the truth. You just keep sleeping, dear Benjamin."

He smelled something odd, almost enough to wake him from his slumber. But then the fog grew heavier and the tree was there, singing gently. He couldn't wake even if he wanted to.

Jekyllyne had drugged him.

"I won't be made a fool again. If he doesn't trust me enough to tell me what he truly did at The Boudoir, then I'll find out myself," Ms. Rielly muttered to herself, stepping from the hansom. "Even if I have to break a promise…"

It was well into the night before she had dared to sneak out of Ainsley Manor. The Lion's Boudoir was highlighted in red against the dark. She located her scalpels and reminded herself that she had stalked a prostitute for the better part of a season once. She pushed thoughts of Moira away and entered the establishment.

She immediately recalled the woman she had badgered when she was here with Reginald the fateful day Alan had passed. She was a stout woman with large hands and a mole on her upper lip. Ibby, if she remembered correctly. Ms. Rielly saw Ibby leaning up against a man with a dark mustache and sauntered over.

"Hello, gent. Might I steal this girl for a spell?"

The man sneered. "Not unless you'd like to fill the spot."

Ibby giggled, but her eyes were threatening. "Girl's too drunk, is all? Go on! Find your own stallion!"

Rielly could swear the woman growled as she walked away.

"You don't seem to belong here," the bartender said, motioning her over. "'Ave a drink? On me?"

Ms. Rielly sat. "Don't usually get patrons of my sort?"

"Not many." He poured something in a glass, red in color. "You look familiar though. Think I saw you pesterin' the ladies once."

She sipped carefully, steering the topic back. "Any special patrons lately? Of the lordship?"

"You definitely don't belong here." The man grinned. "The boss might like you, though. Head on through that back door and wait. She'll come to you."

Rielly did as he said, coming to the room Ainsley had been in just hours before. She refused to rest upon the lounge, opting to stand alongside the painted window. If she scratched at the surface, she imagined she could make a tiny hole to see through but would probably die of dysentery from the contact.

She smiled, thinking of Ainsley coming to a place like this. He probably stood out like a bent nail. She snickered.

"Are you enjoying your night among the shadows?" A beautiful woman came in, stretching her long legs out over the chaise. "Not often I get a customer like you. But, today seems to be the day for people looking for things which ought not to be found."

"Are you the boss? The lady of the house?" Ms. Rielly asked. "My name is—"

"I know who you are, Jekyllyne Rielly. I even know why you're here. I am Calliope." She spread her hands. "How may I help you?"

"I need to know why Ben-Lord Ainsley came here. What did he speak to you about?" She took a defensive stance.

Calliope smirked. "Is his Lordship withholding? Must be for a good reason. And you have nothing I want. Nothing for you to trade."

"I could work for you. For one night, I could be just as charming as any of your best girls. I'll bring in a new kind of client. I've seen how it's done," she offered, jutting out her chin. "I have plenty to trade."

The woman lay back slowly, calculating. "For one night, you are mine. Then I will tell you what your precious lord traded for information."

Her heart pounded, but she agreed. "I'll just get to work then."

"Not quite." Calliope pulled a knife from her robe and fell on Rielly. Before she could scream, a great tear was made in her skirt, half of it falling to a pile on the floor. "Much better. Dress code, you see."

Ms. Rielly swallowed the knot in her throat. "Right."

Her legs were cold despite the stockings, but she felt almost adventurous as she approached men. This was a new opportunity to study the profession. The woman's side of the business she could understand; the male side posed more of a problem. The only struggle she feared tonight was the strength of her curiosity putting off patrons. That, and the slight sense of betrayal to Benjamin. Broken promises and now this, she thought bitterly.

She pasted a smile on her cheeks and sat next to a lonely patron to entertain him. She understood that a place like this, one of "the shadows," was not just a house of selling women. She knew that a lady-run house was something many of the women of the night desired to belong in. A house was safer and required less of the women than those on the streets. They entertained, much like the famed geisha of the Orient. They were actresses in a play every night, pouring drinks, losing at cards to bolster confidence, and feigning interest in each person. A little bit of attention and all the pockets of the world would be emptied.

"May I get you a drink? The red wine tastes of heaven," Ms. Rielly suggested. She had chosen the least harrowing of the options in the room: a short man with thinning hair and a weak look. "I swear you'll fall in love."

"I am already in love," he said sadly. "I don't know why I have come here."

Her eyebrows raised in pleasant surprise. "The heart can sometimes lead us into places we do not mean to go. All it wants is for us to be happy, though. Don't be too hard on it."

"She won't even speak to me. Especially not if she hears of this… indiscretion." He folded under the depression.

She placed a hand on his shoulder. "You have yet to commit anything, my dear. Go home and sleep. Talk to her tomorrow and she will understand. Just make sure you speak only the truth. Women like the truth, even when it may be less than ideal."

The man smiled a little. "You are different. What has led you on a path such is this one?"

She shrugged. "Ironically, a man."

"He doesn't deserve you if he relegates you to live like this."

"I agree," she laughed. "But he is different. Like me."

"Ah," the man nodded, "I do understand that. Perhaps we should both follow your advice then?" He left her with a kiss on the hand.

"I have a spot for you to fill." The man with the mustache yelled across the room, interrupting Ms. Rielly's musings. "Come 'ere, girl. Ibby's gone and left me," he guffawed.

She didn't move, unsure of how to handle such a man. He was already drunk and out of his senses. Not to mention he could probably lift two of her without a hiccup. But she was a deer caught in the predator's unwavering sights and she wasn't about to escape the collision.

"I said come 'ere!" he yelled.

Women around the room jumped, other patrons shaking their heads in disgust. Around a corner Ms. Rielly saw the unmistakable silhouette of Calliope, judging from afar. She

154

stood and made her way over to the man, stopping short a few feet.

This did not deter him, as he swept one large arm out to catch her at the hip and pull her into his lap. "There now! That's better, eh? How's I order a drink for ya, right special?"

"That is my job, I'm afraid," she chided, trying to remain playful. "What is your pleasure, good sir?"

He laughed deep and raucously, swinging her to and fro. "What do ya think?"

Her hips were beginning to ache with his grip on them, she pushed gently away. "Allow me to go get you something nice."

His arm tightened and she almost lost her breath. "You go nowhere, girl. You're 'ere for me!" He laughed again, louder, and jarred her from side to side. "Dance for me!"

She cried out, her heel slipping. Her head was surely made for a hard impact on the floor except for the body in the way. Arms had caught her from the least likely person to appear.

"Michael!" she gasped.

He was glaring at the rowdy man. "Here." He covered her with his coat. "Let us leave."

She stammered. "I can't!"

Calliope materialized at their side, Ibby hiding behind her. "Problems with a loyal patron are strictly prohibited. From woman to woman, you just aren't cut out for the shadows, Ms. Rielly. Get out. The both of you."

"No," she protested. "The information…"

Calliope shifted on her feet, annoyed. "You didn't fulfill your side. But I do like you, so I'll share one thing before you leave." She swirled Ms. Rielly, pressing close to her back to whisper in her ear while she fastened something round her neck. "Your Lord Ainsley is on quite a mission. He kissed me until I told him what he wanted!"

Rielly jerked away from her, face reddening. Michael led her out of the Boudoir and into a waiting carriage. He sat across from her steaming visage.

"Don't believe her," he said. "Persons such as her only speak to tell lies and only lie to profit themselves."

"What do you know?" Ms. Rielly demanded.

"Well, people like her—"

"No, not that," Ms. Rielly clarified. "What do you know about all this? You've clearly been following us. Tell me."

Michael sighed. "I cannot. I have been following you. I apologize. I worried for your safety."

"Well, stop. I have quite enough of that at the manor." She levelled with his eyes. "I am serious. Do not follow me anymore. I thank you for what you did back at the establishment, but it was none of your business."

"I take it Benjamin doesn't know of your moonlighting?"

"You know nothing!" Rielly snapped. "Just leave it alone!"

"I can't."

"Why?"

"Because I care for you," Michael said. "Benjamin may not care enough to keep you off these streets, but I do."

She was at a loss for words. "That's… not how it is."

"However it truly is, I can no longer allow Benjamin to place you in danger." He closed his hands over hers. "Leave him. I can provide accommodations elsewhere, for you and your uncle."

Ms. Rielly inhaled deeply. "Please drop me off at the manor, Sir Peighton."

He let go of her hands slowly, studying her. "Yes, of course. We are already on the way."

The manor came into view, the sunrise casting a light blue hue over the property. Ms. Rielly opened her carriage door, stepping out into the dawn. She glanced back at Michael.

"What are you going to do?" she asked.

He smiled gently. "I am not quite sure, honestly. Just don't ask me to stop following you again."

She chuckled sadly. "Men."

Lord Ainsley was in a panic, waking to the discovery of Ms. Rielly's broken promise. Reginald was still sound asleep from the draught she had concocted. He ran to her room, calling for her, desperate to hear her answer.

The room was empty.

The kitchen was empty, the library empty, and the tearoom empty. By the time he thought to check the theater, he was properly disheveled. He tried to compose himself but failed when he saw her working at the microscope.

He grabbed hold of her, whipping her round. "You're all right! Where were you? Why did you drug Reginald and me?"

"I am sorry," she said. "My plan didn't work out, in any case. I came to no harm, Benjamin. I am fine."

He held her at arm's length, looking her over. "What happened? Why did you act so recklessly against my wishes?"

"Because I can tell when you are lying to me, Benjamin Ainsley!" she accused. "And I tire of it. I tire of everyone trying to protect me from some unknown danger. You should know by now that it is safer to keep me apprised. Not that that excuses my breaking a promise."

He agreed. "I understand, though. I had promised to involve you and I went back on that, as well. I should have shared what I discovered." He prepared himself. "My father may have once worked with a man known only as the Progenitor. He works in black market operations and was one of Alan's connections. If this is true, some of the work my father was doing may not have been completely legal. The foundations on which my family was built may all be a lie. I asked you to take another look at my father's records for that reason."

"I see. And that's why you went to The Lion's Boudoir, because Alan's friends frequent the place," Ms. Rielly said, then blushed. "I... went there to try and find out what you had done. The Lady of the house was... no matter. I found nothing out of the ordinary in your father's records."

Ainsley determined her meaning and also blushed, finally releasing her arms. "Then... we are at an impasse. Once again." He blinked and focused on something near her chest.

She blustered, "What are you staring at?!"

His fingers brushed her skin as he lifted the necklace dangling there. "Where did you get this?"

"What?" She gasped. "The Boudoir... that woman must have put it on me."

Ainsley's eyes filled with affection. "This... this must have been what Alan had buried. As Alan's partner,

Calliope must have known and beat us to it. Or maybe Alan had a contingency plan in place with her."

"What is it?" Ms. Rielly watched as he clicked the locket open before her and used a thumb to wipe at the dirt covering it.

"My mother's," he said.

Inside the oval frame nestled a small black and white snapshot of a woman with a baby. She was smiling gently, the little boy wrapped in her loving embrace. The father was absent, perhaps behind the camera himself.

"She's breathtaking," Ms. Rielly said. "Oh, but you must have this back!" She moved to find the clasp but he stopped her.

"No." He closed the locket and let it slip back into place. "You wear it. Safekeeping. All that matters is that it is home."

"Thank you. I don't know what else to say." She touched it reverently and tried not to meet his eyes. She didn't know what she would do if she did, so she changed the subject. "Does it shed any light on what Alan may have wanted to tell you?"

"I cannot be sure without some time to think on the matter," he admitted. "There are a few possibilities."

"Then back to the Progenitor, what would your father working with this man have to do with all this anyway? Isn't that in the past?" she puzzled over the mystery.

"Perhaps not," he said. "The woman I knew, the Madame, she may have known of my father's business with the Progenitor. If it wasn't him that procured her and Alan's death, then perhaps someone else who knew my father?"

"Coming after you because of something your father did?" The cogs were spinning. "You know who you must ask. You may be able to glean information without revealing that we know about the gun."

"Yes," he admitted. "Reginald served my father for a long time. He had to know. And now, with the necklace in play…" Ainsley stopped, suddenly tracing back through the conversation. "I hope nothing untoward occurred at the Boudoir."

Ms. Rielly grew quiet. "No, nothing. Although, I should tell you Sir Peighton showed. He was following me."

"Implications aside, I think I may have to thank him," Lord Ainsley said. "I hope Reginald will be up to questioning. He was still under your medicine's effects."

"Perhaps the dosing was a bit heavy handed," she said nervously. "I should go check on his progress."

"I'll join you." He started for the stairs, but tottered, losing his footing and bumping into a table.

"Benjamin?" Ms. Rielly took his arm. "Are you alright?"

Sweat ran down his temple, his eyes unfocused. "I can't… Just dizzy." He allowed her to guide him as they slid to the floor, braced against the wall. "Thank you." His chest felt ready to burst.

"Let me examine you." She placed her hands on either side of his face, peering over him. "Your pupils are dilated. Are you experiencing any lightheadedness?"

He smiled. "I can't pinpoint the exact cause at this time."

"Do be serious," she chided. "You cannot charm your way out of this. You are sick and I need to know just how advanced you are." She felt his forehead. "You're warm."

Ainsley leaned his head on her shoulder. "I'm fine."

Ms. Rielly tried not to breathe him in. "I should fetch Reginald. He can help."

"Very true, my lord. How are you feeling?" Reginald appeared, holding a damp cloth.

"Good timing," Ms. Rielly jumped up. "I'm sorry I drugged you, Reginald. I've been trying to ascertain the dosing used on me in Kensington Gardens."

"Do warn me next time should you need volunteers," Reginald said. "I shall make myself scarce."

Lord Ainsley regained his composure. "Reginald, I must ask you something to do with my father's business. Do you know if he kept any clandestine records? Perhaps of partners who may have invested in the Ainsley name?"

"Your father only ever invested in other enterprises," Reginald said. "The late master kept all his records in the study. Why do you ask?"

"I paid a visit to some of Alan's contacts at the Boudoir and found out that Father may have been involved in a black-market group," Ainsley explained. "There is a possibility that someone from those days is targeting people associated with our name, but I cannot know for sure if I'm on the right track without those records. Do you know anything about this?"

Reginald paused, his expression unreadable. "We had to address a few troubles with your father's involvement with the wrong sort. But he never consented to his work being misused for illegal enterprises. I did not figure these misdemeanors from the past had anything to do with the present situation."

"What are you keeping from me, Reginald?"

Ms. Rielly bit her lip, tugging her sleeve. The air was still, the two men measuring each other. She hadn't predicted the turn of events.

"My lord?"

"Reginald, you have served this family faithfully for years. You were my childhood companion and confidant. I trust you, without reservation, with my life." Ainsley finished, "But you must leave this house."

Reginald visibly reacted. "Lord Ainsley—"

"You are henceforth finished serving the Ainsley household." He continued, his tone firm, "You must gather your belongings and leave immediately."

The butler could do nothing but bow.

As he left, Ms. Rielly accosted him, "Benjamin, what are you thinking?"

Lord Ainsley watched the old man's back. "Loyalty... is a peculiar trait, Jekyllyne. If it is true, nothing can best its strength."

Chapter Fourteen

'I Carry Your Heart with Me (I Carry It in My Heart).'
E.E. Cummings

'I cannot fathom what Benjamin is doing. Why would he send Reginald away, just when we might find out what he knows? Could he not order him to share his knowledge?

'Is Reginald still loyal? How could he not be? I cannot imagine the soft, sweet man being anything but the paragon of character I have come to know him as. Yet, why did he dispose of the rifle? I do not want to let it go, but I suppose now it does not matter.

'What are we to do? I throw myself in my work, but my mind wanders back to him. I cannot rein in these feelings. They distract me constantly.

'Benjamin has shut himself in his room.

'What am I to do?'

Ms. Rielly gazed up, as if she could see through the many levels of flooring up into the room where Ainsley had retired. She sighed, her whole body aching. She gathered her papers neatly, looking over all the progression of her writings. But what would they all mean in the end should she fail? Murders and threats be forgotten; how would she cure him? And if she did, would he be done with her, too? Serving faithfully until there was no more need?

She closed the study door behind her as she made her way back to her quarters. It was late, but Lord Ainsley's door had a halo of light around it. She had resigned herself to going to bed until she heard a loud crash.

Ms. Rielly burst through, exclaiming, "Ben!"

She flew to his prostrate form, pulling him into her lap. He was panting, his brow furrowed. "What are you doing here?"

"Benjamin, you are not well. I must get you to the bed," she said.

"You're here. I didn't want to let you in, but here you are," he smiled.

"What?" She examined him. "You're delirious. Oh, if only Reginald were here! I am not strong enough to lift you!"

He took her hand and placed it over his chest, his heart thudding beneath her fingers. "You are here. And I do not want you to leave me."

"I won't," Ms. Rielly said. "I won't leave you, Ben. But I fear you do not even know who I am."

"Lynne," he said, cupping her cheek. "I know who you are."

He extended his neck up so his lips met hers.

She indulged for just a moment, then gently separated from him. "Come, you must sleep."

She managed to heave him into the bed, then fetched him water. She sat by his side, wetting his forehead. He dozed peacefully while the broken halves of her heart warred within her.

***

'I have been making unprecedented strides in the study of Ainsley's sickness. It is as if his kiss awoke something inside me that had long grown cold. I knew this would happen, falling for him, but I cannot fight it any longer. Whether he remembers at all what transpired, I must know how he truly feels. I must know if I am just a temporary replacement for a long-dead truer love.

'His kiss... I am filled with this pressure inside my chest. I fear it will burst forth and cause me to act a fool. But when to ask him? With the burden of recent events?

'I have been working tirelessly since he fell asleep. I cannot stop. I am coming to terms with feelings I never thought possible. Is it morning already?'

Ms. Rielly looked up abruptly from her frantic scribblings. "Ainsley? Is that you?" She had heard what sounded like footsteps. "Benjamin?"

A silhouette formed in the dark.

"You're awake! I am glad you're feeling better," she sighed. "We must speak. I have something I must say, not just regarding what happened with Reginald, but with us."

She stopped. The silhouette did not move or speak. A chill traveled up her spine and her mind raced. She tried to remember where she had hidden her scalpels.

The manor was dark. Lord Ainsley shook the thickness from his head. He had to see Jekyllyne, but something was

165

amiss. The front door was ajar. Rain fell outside and none of the lights were lit.

His bait had once again worked.

He called out in the darkness, "Reginald."

"Yes, Master Ainsley." The butler slipped from the shadows. "At your side."

"Theater. Guns," he said curtly. "We have company."

They parted ways and Ainsley made his way to the study. Over to the trigger behind the limited edition of *Dr. Jekyll and Mr. Hyde*. The way opened and he descended as he had done for years since he first discovered the secret door as a child. Down into the dark theater that once housed his past. Down into the laboratory that now held his future.

"Benjamin!"

The wide room was black save for one lantern. Ms. Rielly stood with a foreign arm hooked around her neck, a man's face just over her shoulder. He held her scalpel to her cheek and the locket in his fist.

"Ben! What's going on? Who is this?" Her eyes were wide with fear and confusion.

"Lord George Connor Ainsley II." His eyes narrowed. "My father."

The man staring back was nearly identical to Benjamin, save the addition of graying hair and wrinkles. He smiled the same smile. "My son. At last you remember."

Benjamin slowly descended toward them. "I was taken aback when Alan suddenly started spouting code in the graveyard. He must have spotted you."

"He was a sharp lad. A bad influence."

"That's why you shot him, yes?" Ainsley asked. "Because Alan had friends, of the professional grave digging sort. He was getting close to the truth."

"Yes. Once Alan realized I had begun liquidating my longtime assets, he grew curious. The Ainsley name has always left a trail." His voice was soft, almost friendly in nature, as if rewarding Benjamin for finding out. "He discovered my empty casket."

Ainsley boots hit the stone floor and he stopped. "And the Progenitor?"

"Yes." He grew quiet, barely moving. "The Progenitor had provided resources in exchange for a hefty endorsement. But my experiments had a price..." he trailed off, cutting Jekyllyne's skin, releasing a drop of blood. His voice became pleading. "Do you know how I have suffered for you? A legacy worth dying for. I was to create unending life! Instead... I created a curse." He was silent, small. "My wife... she put up with me for so long. Understood so little. I had begun my experiments before you were born. We planned for a bright future. She was close to leaving me when she discovered you were growing inside her. Our last chance." He gazed up. "All I wanted was to protect you. Give you everything. Maria."

Ms. Rielly choked on her words. "The garden... when you drugged me. You called me Maria."

"Yes, I won't mistake you for her again," he said, shaking the necklace. "Reginald, my good man, please reveal your part in this. Tell them why you serve me still."

"I do not," Reginald's voice echoed over the stones. "My master knows of my deceit. We discussed it at length. That is when I told him the truth. That I had discovered the rifle to be yours and because of a deep-seated sense of duty, I threw it in the Thames. But my loyalty to my young master won out."

Ms. Rielly gasped. "Then Reginald, he had you leave to draw him out?"

"You killed Madame Tusor. And for what?" Ainsley said, not allowing himself to get pulled off track. "Why did you even return?"

"She was a part of it all, you know. Your innocent governess! Hunting me down, I know it! I had to take care of her before it was too late. Before she ruined us," he argued, almost breathless.

"He's sick," Ms. Rielly spoke. "Just like you. Except his has progressed much further than yours. He might be experiencing side effects akin to paranoia, maybe even hearing voices! He must not realize…"

"Silence!" his father yelled. "I will not be played. My son is not sick. He was born perfect! My work's culmination! I will have no one threaten my legacy. I stopped them and I will stop you from abusing it!"

"My lord!" Reginald suddenly warned. "He's soaked the house with an incendiary! He's clearly gone mad!"

"This isn't the way! Father, you can still end this. Everything will be all right!" Benjamin cried.

"How do you know, my poor son?" George Ainsley asked, his voice filled with sadness. "My sanity comes and goes, even now. And here this girl says you are to go the same way. That I passed onto you the very same death within me. I cannot stomach it."

"Because I trust!" he declared. "I trust in people! I trust in Llyne! Don't you see this is how we carve our futures? I don't care what you may have done in the past. You are my father. And Llyne can help you."

The older Ainsley shook his head. "It is too late. I have made too many mistakes. Reginald, do me one last favor." He drew the scalpel dangerously close to her throbbing artery.

Jekyllyne met Benjamin's meaningful stare. "I can cure you. I will not rest until I do!" She threw her head back with a cry, meeting with her captor's nose full force. He ground out a pained reply and swung the scalpel, slicing hair and dropping the necklace. A shot rang out and Ainsley's head whipped around.

Michael stood with a pistol in his hand, the gun smoking. "Come quickly, Ms. Rielly!"

She obeyed. The elder Ainsley clutched his red shoulder, his face twisted. He stumbled, his eyes fluttering, and crashed into the lamp. He hit the ground as the fire exploded. The flames chased the unseen lines of flammable liquid on the floor, cutting him off from the rest of them.

"My Lord, we must escape!" Reginald emerged from his alcove. "Master Ainsley! We must go!"

Benjamin gazed over the flames to his father's body for a moment. Michael grabbed his arm, snapping him out of it. "Ben!"

They stumbled out of the manor, coughing and eyes watering. The heat was immense. They watched from a safe distance as the house burned, collapsing into itself. The fire brigade was quick to contain it, protecting the surrounding city, but the home was lost.

Michael stood by Benjamin as the men poured water. "You knew I would not let her be hurt." He paused seriously. "I'm sorry for all this. I didn't realize... I hope..."

"I know," he said. "Thank you." He left Michael, patting him on the shoulder, and joined Ms. Rielly.

Her cheek was scabbing over, her hair covered with soot. "I am so sorry, Ben. I do not know how to express..."

He looked past her to the fire. "You expressed it perfectly before. Perhaps we all wish we knew our loved ones better than anyone else. That man... was not my father. My father died in a carriage crash years ago. He died a gentleman."

She held onto his arm. "Ben..."

"I am thinking this is a good opportunity to give you a proper lab," he said. "We'll build it atop the ashes. Right, Reginald?"

"Yes, Master Ainsley," he smiled.

Jekyllyne smiled too. "I suppose I do have more work to do. Are you sure I can stay?"

"Wouldn't have it any other way, Lady Rielly."

Six Months Later

Ms. Rielly answered the bell when it rang, "Michael, good to see you!" She was chipper and her hair was cut short in a becoming bob. "I'd lead you into the tea room, but we do not quite have one yet." She laughed. "I'll fetch Benjamin."

Michael thanked her kindly and waited in the entryway, nervously twirling his hat in his hands. He could see that the manor had been under constant construction since the fire. The outside was completed, but the inside was still in progress. Michael could discern a certain influence in the new iteration of its walls and furniture. He smiled to himself.

"Michael. How are you?" Benjamin rounded a corner, his collar dusty and unbuttoned. "I apologize for not sending word sooner. We have been especially busy."

Michael took his hand in a firm shake. "No matter. I have had other things tying me up as well."

"Work for Her Majesty never stops," Ben said.

"True," Michael replied. "I thought you would want to know what had occurred with our investigation into the Progenitor."

Ainsley braced himself. "Yes."

"After your father's… passing," he stumbled over the right words, "word came to us that the Progenitor had begun to empty his estates. We infiltrated a well-known compound of his, but we found nothing useful. Our contacts have ascertained his location: America." Michael paused. "I will be travelling forthwith to resume following the trail from there."

He let this sink in. "You must tell Llyne. She will want to know where you have gone off to."

Michael chuckled. "And I had feared she hated me."

"Women's hearts are a marvelous and agonizing organ," Ainsley said. "I find myself suffering more and more from it each day." He smiled wide.

"You seem happy," Michael stated. "At one time, I thought of nothing else except your suffering. But recently I feel changed. I feel… happy that you only suffer what the heart gives." He shrugged. "I had hoped to visit more, but I must leave for the States soon."

Benjamin nodded. "Perhaps with my new business I shall pay you a visit. Movies cannot be made without broader audiences."

"*Movies?*" He was shocked, but in a pleasant way. "A new direction for us all." Michael opened the door, but hesitated. "Benjamin… When we examined some of the items we found at the compound, we did find something of note. There was a file marked 'Finances.' With your father's name on it. It was badly damaged, but I was able to discern some information."

Ainsley stilled.

He continued, "Your father was paying the Progenitor only for supplies for his work. He never did become

172

involved with shadier dealings. It was only a matter of time until the Progenitor wanted access to his project. Your father did not want it falling into the wrong hands and refused. He devised a plan to fake his own death but did not foresee your mother falling victim to it as well. By that point, his mind was probably too far gone." Michael took Benjamin's shoulders in his hands, looking squarely into his eyes. "The point is your father was a good man. He didn't intend for any of this fallout from his indiscretions. Good intentions, though…"

"Thank you," Ainsley said quietly, "for everything."

Michael scoffed. "Just did my duty. Send my best to Jekyllyne. And if you bring her with you to America, all gentlemanly bets are off. I will take her from you."

Ainsley closed the door. "You can try."

Epilogue

'Lord Ainsley was born into a small family. All his parents ever wanted for their only son was for him to live. The Ainsley Manor is much changed since that boy grew into a man.

'He went searching for his fortune, lost comrades, first loves. He suffered the world for its ambition and came home only to discover the man he'd been was gone. A stranger stood in his place.

'But that's what happens when you live. Although, some experiences are not the same as others. And I do not recommend recreating the particular events of this one!

But all is well just as he said it would be. Life is relatively quiet. For now.'

Ms. Rielly finished penning her sentence and smiled. The mansion was even more expansive than before, with a unique lab under construction, just for her. Slowly but surely, the manor was becoming home.

All was put to rest. And now I can finally put down my pen, before Llyne notices I've been writing of her. I feel as if my writings have only just begun.

Lord Benjamin Ainsley III